The Goodbye Station

A novella
by Gracie Stella Cook

Back Cover photograph by Patty Bowman

Author Page sketch by author.

ISBN: 9798675073597

HATS OFF

TO

VETERINARIANS, ZOOKEEPERS, FARMERS,

RESCUERS, CAREGIVERS, GUARDIANS,

SCIENTISTS, CONSERVATIONALISTS,

AND ALL OTHERS WHO GIVE OF THEMSELVES

FOR

ANIMALS

THE GOODBYE STATION

THE GOODBYE STATION

We were always on the outer edge of existence…the last place to stop before moving on forever.

They only came to us when there was nowhere else in this world to go. Sometimes they stayed a long time with us, but other times their visits were hardly any length at all. And all were only temporary. We always knew we would say goodbye.

But we never turned any of them away; no matter what condition they were in, they were welcome. Most times, someone somewhere had decided they weren't worth saving. But if Pa heard about them, it wasn't like that.

Ruby used to say, "Lordy, Lordy, look at this here…now this is sad," every time a new charge arrived, as if each was somehow in worse shape than the ones before. But we did what we could, did something for every one of them. Especially Ruby. She was so good with them, even the ones who made trouble for us. The problem ones actually seemed to like her best, probably sensed a kindred spirit. She said her soul was failing, same as their bodies.

Understand, Ruby wasn't with us yet when Pa first started to take these poor creatures in. No, she came to us later, after Pa put an ad for help needed in the local paper and the country store in town.

Seems like we've known Ruby forever but it's only been for not even three years. Pa's been doing the caretaking for going on five years now. Ruby's kind of a pistol but she works hard, always has. Out of the three of us helpers, she's the best worker. Pa is always saying that and we know it, too. And we all know they like her the best.

Every morning they're all standing there, looking for her. Waiting for Ruby to bring them their breakfast. Best part of the day.

For us. For them…the horses.

Ruby likes to say she has a system, for everything really, but especially for the meals. She always feeds the most forward ones first. It keeps them busy and they don't beat up on the others, plus the meek ones don't seem to mind waiting, as long as they get something. And they always do. Ruby sees to it.

Lately, I get to feed the timid ones. It's my favorite job because they're so grateful. And so patient, waiting and watching me. There's four or five of them now that stand in a little group nearby so they can see me while I get their meals together.

It takes a minute extra since the older ones need to have softer food, easier for them to chew. I use a spray bottle of water and spritz their hay just a little, to make it even softer. Feels good feeding them, it's what they look forward to most, Ruby says. Maybe this is how Ma feels when she cooks for the whole crew of us humans. Sometimes I wonder, though. Maybe she'd just as soon cook only for herself and to hell with the rest of us. But maybe that's just me, not thinking very much of people.

Ruby always says the three of us, herself and Ma and me, we like critters more than people. She's right about me, for sure.

****

I call them that, but I'm not really blood to Pa and Ma. Never was. They took me in when I was ten years old, after Social Services called Ma about me. And long months after Ma had the miscarriage that lost them their real daughter.

Right after that happened, Ma screamed and cried and said she wanted to die, too. That's what Gary told me, years later, when I was sixteen and started working with him and Pa out in the fields on the farm. He said the doctor had also told Pa it would be physically dangerous for Ma to try to have another baby anyway. She had already been over the hill for a first try. Next time she could die of a stroke or a heart attack.

Gary told me that after the doctor said that, Pa got himself snipped so Ma would never get pregnant again. Gary said he would never go that far; he'd just stay away from Ma. But, like Ruby told me later, Gary acts like he's barely older than me, and ignorant besides. I guess he was lucky we were out of hearing distance from Pa when he said all that to me.

What I never told Gary, or anybody else, or talked about with Ma and Pa, although they probably heard it from the child welfare folks, was anything about when I got taken from the house in the town where I was born. Not the town the farm is closest to, but another town, many miles away. They took me out, and an ambulance came and took my baby brother away, but I'll never know what happened to the rest of them.

I'm over nineteen now, and I don't think about any of it much, but every once in a while, I remember the anger house.

Both of them screaming at us. Him beating on Her, and then Her whaling on us young ones. Him, after losing another job because of drink, yelling and cursing about how we were too many mouths to feed and too much trouble all around. Her saying I was a ugly thing for a girl and the only reason not to drown me being I was sturdy and strong so I could work; too bad I was too dumb and lazy to be good for anything.

And that night, the last one. With me too paralyzed with horror, too scared to move, almost too beat down to watch but unable to look away. He was out of his mind with rage. When He threw Her up against the sink, she grabbed the liquor bottle from the counter and smashed my baby brother in the face with it. The poor little kid was sitting on the kitchen floor and screaming with a face full of blood.

I'll never know who called the cops, maybe our neighbor on the other side of the duplex, but cops came. They put the baby in an ambulance and took me and my older brother out of the house. Because I was adopted by the farm folks, Ma and Pa, from another county, I never found out what happened to my brothers. I hope they made it out, like I did. I really do. Don't know what happened to those others, those I call Him and Her. I like to think they're in jail, but I don't care enough to find out. Why would I.

Anyway, I came here to the farm and I've been here for almost ten years. Kind of feels like it's all I've ever known. It's quiet here mostly, with all the animals: barn cats, that weird looking dog, and the horses. We got chickens, too, but they make a little noise at times. Our rooster is pretty tame though, and not too loud even when he crows. Ma told me he's the sweetest rooster she's ever met.

His name is Hombre, but lucky for us and the hens, and even the cats, he doesn't live up to it. He'll even come to you if you call him by name or cluck pretty loud or whistle. Ma and Pa can whistle but I can't. Pa tried to teach me; he was patient, but I couldn't do it. When I gave up, he just laughed and said to never mind. I'm glad he was the one that tried to teach me cause when I give up on something, Ma doesn't always laugh, and she looks pretty stern.

Everybody here on the farm knows Ma is the boss. And she is one huge woman. Not so tall maybe, but she is really stout and fat. Gary used to always say that Ma is a 'doublewide' and one time, Ruby heard him say it. That was the last time he ever said that out loud since Ruby threatened to hit him in the snout if she ever heard it said again. Gary's the only one here more afraid of Ruby than he is of Ma. Ruby is not as fat as Ma, but she's taller and has big strong bones and a big fist. And she's whole worlds louder than Ma.

That's the thing. This farm was almost too quiet before Ruby joined us. I don't talk much; Pa only talks when he needs to; and Ma hardly says anything unless you ask her a question. Gary does talk pretty much, most times when he should keep his mouth shut, but when he's working, he stays quieter to conserve energy because he never seems to have enough.

But Ruby talks, sometimes all day long. Pa says he doesn't know how she can work so hard and still talk so much. But she does. She has something to say about almost everything that happens, everyone she sees, including the critters (as she calls them), plus all the folks from anywhere nearby that the rest of us might know about, and some famous people we don't know but might have heard of.

She has a nice voice though. On the deep side, what some call husky, and never screechy. I like to listen to her. So do Pa and Gary; they haven't said so, but I can tell. Plus, she's funny and interesting, some of the crazy things she says. The sound keeps us working well. One day Gary said to her, "Can't never take you fishing though, Ruby. You'd scare the fish away."

"Why in the living hell would I want to go fishing with you in the first place?" is what she said back to him.

Pa and I were laughing and Gary's face turned red, but then he started laughing, too. Ruby's language is kind of rough, but the three of us, Gary, Pa and me, we like it. It makes us laugh a lot. Ma frowns when she hears some things Ruby says, so Ruby tries to 'cool it' when Ma's around. According to Ruby, that's out of courtesy and respect for Ma.

See, Ray Keegan, that's Pa's name, never owned this farm. Ma's people owned it; it was in their family for years and years. The Espinosa's came up here from Mexico long ago and bought the land before Ma's father was even born. Ma, called Dulce, was the oldest of the farm's fourth generation living here.

She and her father had a special relationship. Her father loved her more than he loved his other, younger kids because Dulce's mother Alicia died in childbirth and he had been crazy in love with Alicia. Some men would have hated the surviving child, but he didn't lay blame on her. Instead he clung to her, favoring her and depending on her at the same time.

Because Dulce loved the farm. She fell in love with the land, the animals, the farmhouse, the whole way of life, when she was just a little girl. And she stayed that way, even as an adult. Old Mrs. Espinosa, her grandmother, taught Dulce to cook and clean the house and do the washing, ironing, sewing and mending of the clothes and tending to the chickens.

Dulce was so good at cooking that she grew up stout and fat, but not at all lazy. Nobody could ever call her lazy. She did the cooking and housework, fed the chickens, farm cats and Amory, the big old draft horse her father used to plow the crop fields. In planting season, she went out to the fields and led the big blonde horse back and forth while her father guided the plow. She even helped in the back-acreage's apple orchard when it was time to pick the apples.

Her father had remarried and he and his second wife had four children, but none of them was as invested in the farm as Dulce and her father. Her three half-sisters all married and moved away before they turned twenty-five, and when the youngest left to start her own family in a distant town, Dulce's stepmother went with her. The only boy in the family enlisted in the military, met his future wife while they were both in the service, and later settled down in another state where his wife's family lived.

On the day Dulce turned forty, only she, her father and her abuela were living in the farmhouse. Her father trusted his daughter would always live in the house his grandfather built and would never leave the farm. One of his biggest comforts in life was that Dulce had never paid any attention to boys, including the boys and men he hired to help with apple harvest.

Then, after his mother had passed away and during the year Dulce turned forty-five, he hired 34-year old Ray Keegan. Dulce only needed one look at Ray, and the life her father envisioned for her changed forever.

Before that year's apple harvest was over, Dulce had

married a migrant farm worker, more than ten years her junior. A man basically a stranger to her and her father. Although the marriage was hard for her father to accept, and he shed private tears over it, he did not change his will. After he died, Dulce would have the farm for as long as she lived.

But then he regretted that his favorite daughter had not married when she was younger so she could have had children she could will the farm to. He doubted she could produce any heirs now. Her father hoped Dulce might, when she was older, will the Espinosa farm to her younger half-brother, which could restore the family name. But he realized there was small chance of that happening since her brother may not want the farm and even more since his daughter was in love with Ray Keegan, who would probably survive Dulce and the farm would someday be his.

And shortly, due to decades of physically strenuous work with little rest and a lifetime of keeping constant worries mostly to himself, Dulce's father succumbed to a fatal heart attack weeks before her miscarriage. He would never know she was pregnant when Ray married her.

Ray comforted her after her father's death and right away again after she lost their only baby. Dulce loved him from the get-go, and she knew his kindness before they married, but folks from the surrounding farms and the town's people nearby were suspicious of this unfamiliar man from nowhere they knew, who was suddenly running the Espinosa farm just months after he arrived. Some of them wondered if he married Dulce so he could live and work on the farm.

But he never paid them any mind. He just went about the business of taking care of his wife, the land, the chickens and barn cats and Rufus, the red roan Brabant draft horse Dulce had known from her thirties. Ray planted trees and built shelters for shade in the pastures close to the barn and farmhouse so Rufus could stay dry in the winter and cool in hot summers on days he wasn't being worked in the fields.

Ray kept Dulce's father's pickup truck in good shape and drove it into town to buy supplies, groceries and feed. He was always easygoing and polite in town and pretty soon people started to take to him. After a few months, when her mourning had eased up a little, Dulce went with him. Seeing how relaxed they were with each other helped other folks trust Ray more.

Another thing that broke the ice for Dulce's husband was word that got around farms in the area and in town, words from young Gary Pepper, praising Ray. The Peppers' farm bordered the Espinosa farm on the northeast and about a month after Dulce married Ray, Gary Pepper, the youngest son, then only around sixteen, showed up next door to his home and asked Ray if he had any at least part-time work.

Gary lived on his family's farm but did not want to work there since he couldn't get along with his oldest brother Bob, who was in the process of taking over farm operation from their old man Jimmy Pepper. Bob couldn't be bothered with Gary's loose tongue and lazy work ethic, and he told Gary so.

So, Gary took himself one farm over and started working with the man he called Mr. Keegan. Ray gradually broke Gary of calling him 'mister,' and eased him into work on the farm. When Gary showed himself to be pretty nervous around big Rufus (the Pepper farm used a tractor), Ray taught him how to clean the draft horse's harness and the handheld plow used in planting the Espinosa farm's row crops.

Gary also learned how to muck out the horse stall in the big barn; Rufus was stabled inside at night and during cold, stormy weather. After a few months of Gary mucking out, Ray told him that since he was doing a good job, and if and when he got over his nervousness around Rufus, he could learn to groom, harness and lead the horse and help with feeding him. If Gary wanted to learn to master these other chores, Ray himself would clean the stall.

It only took two days for Gary to decide he was no longer afraid of the big red roan animal with black mane, tail and legs. It didn't hurt that Rufus was as calm, gentle and patient as he was very large. And it sure helped that Gary was tired of every day scooping up horse manure and soiled stall bedding and pushing it out to the compost heap in a heavy wheelbarrow.

Shortly after Gary started helping Ray weekends, summers, and late afternoons, changes came gradually to the Espinosa farm. That's when Pa and

Ma adopted a child from the child welfare folks. That was me, and although I didn't want to, Ma and Pa both insisted I attend school in the county. Since Gary was still going to class at the same school, he used to walk me to the bus stop and ride with me to the schoolhouse. In the afternoons Pa would drive the truck over and pick me up at the bus stop since Gary left school early due to his work/study program, the same kind I was in after I turned sixteen.

If not for Gary, and later Ruby, I'd never have known any of the history around Pa and Ma and the Espinosa farm. I never talked with Pa and Ma about it, and they never talked to me about the past. Theirs or mine.

I only learned what I know of their story because Gary heard tell from his people and farm neighbors and folks in town. And because Ruby made it her business to find out everything she could about Pa and Ma and the farm and its surrounds from neighbors and townspeople she talked to. She also made it her business to talk to everybody she came across, and listen to them also. Especially to anything they might say about Pa. And one time she hinted to me that she heard about Pa from the city, from before Ruby herself ever ventured out to rural life.

That time Ruby said to me, "You know, your Pa has been to the rodeo a couple times, I'm pretty sure."

I said, "Well, he's experienced with horses; everybody says that. Did he ride broncs? Do you know?"

"No," Ruby laughed when she corrected me, "not that kind of rodeo, not the rodeo with horses and cows. Maybe he did that, too, but I'm talking about a different kind of rodeo. The city kind. He spent some time down south, you know. Los Angeles. I lived there for a while. Saw a picture of him once. In the newspaper. Ray Keegan…you never forget that face."

Her voice faded a little on that last line. She sounded wistful, like she was remembering. It made me confused. And a little mad.

"I hope you tell me what you meant by all that. Why was Pa's picture in the paper?"

Ruby squinted at me. "Nah, girl," she said. "You don't need to hear about anything like that. Sorry I brought it up. Forget I said anything."

She got up from sitting in the grass with me, and she walked away. I sat for a minute and decided she was right. Decided I didn't need to bother. I didn't want to know. Might be lies anyway. People tell lies, all of them do. That's what I know.

****

The horse rescue started when I was almost fifteen and Pa got a call from the veterinarian who saw to large animals in our area. He told Pa he was trying to save an older part-Arab mare that needed surgery to remove a stone (enterolith in vet speak) and her owner gave up on her. Desperate to find someone to not only pay for the operation but willing to give her a good home and take care of her, he remembered the kind treatment Pa gave to Rufus, our old plowing horse.

Since the vet doctored Rufus, giving him regular vaccinations and exams and such, and he knew Pa was looking to retire the big horse and find a younger animal to take on the farm work, he understood how much Pa really loved horses. Plus, he would take any excuse to get to see and talk to Pa.

But the main reason the vet asked and the reason Pa said yes was the old mare herself. She was a special twenty-something girl. A very dark, what they call a liver chestnut color, with a big white star on the forehead of her dishy Arab face, she looked like a chocolate fantasy horse, and her name was Mirabella. Her personality was golden in spite of too long standing in a small stall, broken by episodes of too much hard riding and too little attention and care from the owner who refused surgery for her, even though she had the money to pay, and told the vet to put her down since the mare was already old.

The vet, Dr. Spelling, felt like he couldn't do it. So, he called Pa, and Pa said he'd talk to Ma and call back. Ma said yes, Pa called back and told the doctor to go ahead with the operation and Pa would drive to the animal hospital and take care of the financial paperwork.

Pa asked Ma and Gary and me to plan on feeding Rufus and the chickens and barn cats since he might be back late; it was a pretty long drive. Anyway, Ma and I always gathered the chickens to their coop inside the big barn and fed them, but Gary did at least stay and help out with Rufus and the cats.

Mirabella's surgery went well. She recovered and came home with us, and from her arrival was a fine companion for Rufus, before and after his retirement. We mostly call her "Mira" these days. She's still with us now; she's at least twenty-eight and Rufus is in his thirties, and they still hang together. They get the softest timothy hay we have and lots of good grazing.

Sometimes when Pa, Gary and I were working out in one of the crop fields, I'd look back and watch Ma interrupt hanging out the wash so she could go into the pasture with Mira and Rufus and love up on them. Those were the times Ma would smile, when she was with the horses, or the chickens, or house or barn cats, or more recently, with the weirdest dog anybody's ever seen, that dog, "Persk." Yep, a true mutt, and another rescued critter on the farm.

The second horse to receive a forever home on the farm was the easiest case we took in. This time the horse's owners called Pa and asked if we could give their beloved hunter/jumper Thoroughbred a retirement home. They said Dr. Spelling had told them about us and we might be the answer to their prayers.

Their horse, with stable name "Freckles," won ribbons and trophies for the family's young riders and they all loved him, but needed to retire him since at eighteen he started having some chronic tendonitis. Dr. Spelling had treated Freckles with liniment and wrapping his leg and ordering stall rest. But although he was moving sound as he got better, the family decided not to risk putting him back to work.

They couldn't afford to retire him plus buy a new show pony, but they were determined to find a really good permanent home where he could take life easy in pasture with other horses for company and people who appreciated and cared for him.

They trailered Freckles all the way from another county to our farm; the whole family, parents, a daughter and a son, came along to help him settle into his new home. Pa would first put him in a small, level, mostly dirt lot with a little grass and within sight of Rufus and Mira, but separated. That was so he couldn't eat too much grass when he wasn't used to it, so he wouldn't get up to speed, frisking around, and so he got to know the other horses at a distance.

When the Missus of the family led Freckles out of the trailer and handed his leather lead to Pa, everybody on the whole place fell in love with him, including the other horses. Sixteen hands high of refined and elegant confirmation, a shiny chestnut coat with a golden sheen, two white socks in front with a white stocking behind on one leg, and a funny face that was just out and out cute.

That face showed off the Arabian blood way back in his lineage. A lot of the cuteness, though, was in his smiling eyes and in the three brown spots inside his face-long squiggly blaze. Easy to figure that the spots on his white nose gave him his nickname, the only name we ever knew for him.

Pa led Freckles into his pen, closed the gate, and led him into the center before he took his fine halter and lead-line off. Pa backed a couple of steps while Freckles looked all around and breathed in the air. Pa walked back outside, closing the gate again, and offered the halter and lead back to Freckles' former family but they declined.

We all watched Freckles walk to the fence nearest to the pasture with the other horses. Then he let out the shrillest, funniest, high-pitched whinny I'd ever heard, and everybody laughed. That was the essence of the creature that stole my heart: the face and grace of a prince with the personality of a puppy dog. Friendly from day one, Freckles got along with people and animals, just a happy, easygoing boy. And he's still the same.

We wish it could be like that for all our rescues, but as Ruby says, it just can't be. Many of the horses we took in were in really bad shape from injuries, abuse or neglect, or a combination. Several of them were only with us for a few months.

One old horse, a gray gelding with a sad story, hung on for over four years. He was found almost starved at a place where the elderly couple who lived there fell on hard times themselves. The husband died and the wife lost her mind and her money and couldn't keep up the house, the property or their two horses. The other horse had a bad injury and had to be put down, but the gelding we took in survived and slowly got better.

His name was Gun Powder, a name every one of us hated, but he knew that name. Since he was pretty much all white with age, Pa dropped the "Gun" and took to calling him "Powder," and that was better. At first, he was extremely weak and we had to feed him up very carefully, a little at a time but often.

As Powder got stronger, Pa put him in pasture with Freckles. Both sweethearts, those two were the best of friends and would graze quietly side by side for hours every day. Powder loved standing in the sun, and when it stayed light until late, you had to be careful if you went to halter him and bring him to the barn. At least once, when I went to get him, I didn't realize he was standing there sound asleep, and I startled him since I didn't speak, just walked up and touched him on the neck. He made a funny sound and shook a little but then he nuzzled me. That was my bad; Pa had always cautioned me to speak first when I approached any horse. Next time I said his name before I touched.

When she first joined us on the farm, Ruby got the biggest kick of those two pasture pals. She'd holler at them before she even opened their gate. Making her voice higher, she'd call out, "Free-reckles! Pow-DER!" and they'd lift up their heads and trot right over to her. She never needed to walk to them; they always came to her.

One morning, five months or so ago, when we were in the barn getting the horses out for their day in pasture, I saw Ruby and Pa whispering together in front of Powder's stall. It surprised me when Ruby haltered Freckles and led him out of the barn. Usually she would also halter Powder and take them out together.

I closed back up the stall I was opening; by the time I turned around, Pa was standing beside me. He put his arm around me, he doesn't often do that, and he told me in a soft voice that old Powder was gone. He said Powder had died of old age in his sleep, and Pa believed he was really old since Powder had to have been already going on thirty when we took him in.

Honest, I tried hard not to cry, but tears were on my face before I even knew it. Pa hugged me close for a second, and whispered to me that Powder had died happy, but suddenly I cried out, "What about Freckles? He can't be alone out there, can he?" Ruby came back into the barn and Pa let me go.

Ruby put a hand on my shoulder and said to me, "Don't you worry, girl, Freckles is out with Rufus and Mira. And don't you fret about old Powder. He died in his sleep and that's the best any of us can hope for. Now, you come with me. That lazy-ass Gary just got here and he'll help Ray with the horses today. And that son of a bitch Persk can stay with the guys, but you and I are gonna dry dishes and take care of the chickens and cats with your Ma, so come on, now."

She hustled me out of the barn and toward the kitchen

to meet up with Ma before Gary could see that I had tears on my face. Ruby gave me her bandana and let me dry up those tears before Ma could see. While Gary was walking into the barn, Ruby whispered to me that Pa would tell Ma about Powder, so we, she and I, shouldn't say anything. I asked if Pa would tell Gary, too, and Ruby nodded yes. All of us loved Powder, Gary especially maybe, since he had never been afraid of that quiet little old horse, grateful for anything we did for him.

Powder came to us in starvation poor condition due to neglect, Mirabelle because she needed surgery her owner wouldn't pay for, Freckles had a sore tendon and needed to retire, and Rufus was, in Ruby's words, 'pensioned' since he was over thirty after working on the farm for many years.

Other horses came and passed on, some old and arthritic and unable to be ridden, some used and ill, due to physical wounds or abuse, some neglected and unwanted. Sometimes people wanted to help them but couldn't afford to, and sometimes those who owned them didn't care, couldn't cope, or wanted to trade in for something 'better.'

These days we have seven rescue equines living on the property. Besides Mira and Freckles, we have Rainey, Lurcher, Teddy, Taz, and Lizette. Rainey, a brown Quarter type mare, has Navicular; she's the only horse Pa puts shoes on, front feet only. The rest he just trims their feet.

We figure Lurcher must have been named from some sort of zombie TV series or movie. He kind of looks like a zombie, but doesn't exactly act like one. He's a biggish, rangy, spavined gelding with a large head and a weird colored coat. We're pretty sure he's part Appy cause of his eyes, which we have to treat with medicine sometimes. We also put stuff on his face to protect him from sunburn, like we do on Freckles' partly pink nose.

Lurcher had been a rent horse. He burned out on his job and started balking and refusing to move, or if he did move, he went backwards. He was slated for the meat market when some kind people, who used to rent-ride him before he quit giving what he didn't have to give anymore, paid the man who ran the rent string a little something and gave Lurcher to us. At sixteen he's one of our younger horses and he might be with us for a long time, just grazing and relaxing in his leisure. But he can be a hazard to the rest of us.

Lurcher's really not at all mean but he has no ground manners whatsoever. Pa tries to teach him but it's anything but easy. Ruby said she and Pa figure Lurcher's been prodded and poked, and smacked and jerked around, and yelled at and maybe even beat on for most of his life, so his attitude is to never mind what anybody does, he'll do as he wants and ignore everyone else. And he's extra pushy about his food, both with any other horses near him at feeding time and with whoever puts the hay out.

Only Pa and Ruby can handle Lurcher. Gary avoids

him altogether and if I try to halter him, it doesn't usually work. He swings his big head around and I can't buckle the halter on him. I get frustrated and he gets away with acting stupid. Usually Ruby just takes over for me. He listens best to her, plus she's tall.

Nowadays, Lurcher's turned out with Rainey. She seems to like him so she doesn't even care if Lurcher gets fed first. And, like Ruby pointed out, Rainey doesn't give a 'hoot or holler' about anything he does. She just ignores him when he's stupid. If Lurcher tries to get too pushy with her, Rainey lopes over to the other side of their field, making him have to use energy to catch up or keep his nonsense to himself.

Teddy came to us about two years ago; Taz, short for Tasmanian Devil, had already lived on the farm six months before, but we weren't sure we'd be able to keep him. Even Pa considered giving up on Taz. None of us ever thought about giving up on Teddy, but we weren't sure he'd make it; not even Dr. Spelling had high hopes for poor Teddy.

The day Teddy arrived at the farm was the day I saw anger, maybe all the way to hatred, on Ma's face. It took Teddy a good ten minutes to back out of the trailer. He could barely move. Pa had backed the trailer up so Teddy would have soft ground to walk on, but everybody watching could see that the horse's front feet were sore.

Dr. Spelling had told Pa and Ma Teddy's story. He'd been a good horse, easy to ride and eager to please, but bad luck when he was eleven paired him with ignorant owners who rode him too fast, long, and hard on hard ground and kept him overly grained up so they could get more speed out of him. He got laminitis, and the vet where he was stabled treated him and told them stall rest and no riding at all. They did not listen. He foundered and the veterinarian chastised the owners; they shouted back that they were through with a horse they couldn't ride, and Dr. Spelling got a call from the stable owner looking to find help for the horse.

As Teddy minced over to dirt Pa had wetted to make softer, Ma stepped over and took the lead from Pa. Her mouth was set grim, but when her anger faded, her eyes were kind. She spoke to Teddy while he stood in the pen and looked around while Pa brought him lovely timothy hay and filled his water trough.

What none of us would ever forget, not Pa or Ma, or Ruby, Gary, or me, or Dr. Spelling, who was there to treat Teddy and help him settle in, we'd none of us forget that although Teddy had trouble walking, his eyes showed he wanted to live.

During months and months, it was a long, slow climb for that sweet little bay horse. Pa pastured him in a small field with not too much grass, soft footing, and a fence in common with the pasture holding Freckles and Powder. The only human-guided exercise Teddy did was walking slowly out to his field in the morning and back to the barn at night. Nobody ever rushed him, and when he was let out, he only needed to move when he felt like it. Shelter, hay and water, and a little grass to nibble on were all there for him, and friendship was just a glance away on the other side of the fence.

Pa would say he figured the only reason we kept Taz was that Ruby couldn't help but like him. He said what he couldn't figure out was why he took the soured animal in, in the first place. But he was joking; he liked the horse, too.

A guy Pa talked to in town told Pa he had bought a horse at auction that he had to give away somehow. The horse seemed sound and strong enough to ride all day, but the horse was also dangerous to people and other critters. The horse would bite, kick and charge at unpredictable times, and had recently attacked one of their goats that got into his paddock. If a couple of ranch-hands hadn't seen it happen and managed to interfere, the goat might have been killed.

Besides that, as the guy told Pa, Tasmanian Devil had, even after he'd been ridden for hours the day before, bucked something fierce with him, and when he stayed on, tried to pin his leg against the corral fence. His owner decided right then that he could not control this animal and the horse had to go.

Before Pa took his truck and trailer to go collect this beast at the ranch, he told Ruby and me we could go along but we were to watch only. Very firmly, he instructed us to refrain from getting near the horse. He said Ruby, and only Ruby, could help him close the trailer door after the horse was loaded, but that was it. We were going with him only to learn, and that was all.

"I want you both to understand what I'm going to tell you now. We have room for another horse, and we're trying to save this guy, but there's a chance, a pretty big chance, we won't be able to keep him. But that would be my responsibility, my decision, and maybe, my failure. Mine, only. This monkey means serious business, and for us to succeed, we've got to watch every step we take with him. Understood?"

That's what Pa said to us and we knew he meant every word. While Pa got the trailer ready, I told Ruby that whenever Pa uses the word 'monkey,' it always means something is a challenge for him. She nodded and said, "Some fine day, your Pa will use 'monkey' for me," and then she winked at me. I had to cut my giggle off short so Pa wouldn't hear it. But I didn't know exactly what she meant, and I didn't ask.

When we got to the ranch, Pa got the owner's permission to turn the horse out and let him blow off steam before being loaded into our trailer. As soon as we saw Tasmanian Devil, we knew why the guy giving him to us bought him at a kill pen auction.

He was what they call a tri-color, bay, black and white, 'Medicine Hat' Paint, and looked like probably part Quarter Horse and part Mustang, a sturdy and handy gorgeous looking horse. Later, Ruby told me that looking at Taz, a person might think, 'I want to ride that horse.' But then, if that unhinged look showed up in his eyes, if he pinned his dark ears flat back, and if he started snaking his head around to get a biting angle, and if he let out with one of his high-pitched squeals of rage, a body might think, 'better not.' And be right.

With the prior owner and Ruby and I watching, Pa led Taz over to a round pen on the property. Pa used a classic correct two-handed hold on the lead-line, firm but not tight. Taz behaved fine while Pa hooked the gate shut and then hand walked him to the center of the pen. When Pa took his halter off, he stood there quietly facing Pa until Pa stepped aside and flicked the old plastic-weave carriage whip, he had picked up at a tack sale, towards the ground near the gelding's hindquarters but without touching him.

The horse trotted obediently out of the middle of the pen but stopped short of going too close to the outside rail. He pawed the dirt and got down and rolled all the way over. Then he sprang to his feet and exploded, galloping and bucking around the pen with Pa watching him from the center.

After a minute or so of letting loose in one direction, Taz slowed to a walk, then turned toward the center, and Pa, who moved to the horse's right, pointed the carriage whip at his right side and motioned with his hand for the horse to go left to the rail so he would reverse direction. Pa said, "reverse," out loud in a clear, calm voice, but Taz hesitated. Pa tapped the whip on the ground on Taz's right and repeated the word 'reverse' and this time it worked. Taz tracked to the right along the rail and Pa told him, "good boy."

The owner mentioned to Ruby and me that the horse occasionally charged at people, but he was behaving well today, so maybe this 'handover' was meant to be. He said he was losing money on this varmint but he liked the horse too much to sell him in case someone who bought him got hurt and Tasmanian Devil ended up back at auction and sold to the out-of-state meat market. He said he hoped he was doing the right thing.

"You sure are," Ruby said confidently to him. "He'll get turned out on his own in pasture on the farm with other horses in sight but not in harm's way. Ray will work with him and he won't let anybody else handle him unless he trains the handler and they're not scared of the horse."

"Well, that's good," the man answered, "but 'Devil' is unpredictable sometimes. That's mainly why I'm giving up on him. And I'm no novice, sweetheart."

We watched Ray halter Taz and lead him out of the round pen while Ruby reassured the previous owner that Ray was aware of the horse's behavior problems. Then she turned her face away from him and towards me. She made a face at me and I knew why. She hates to be called sweetheart by strangers, maybe by anybody. I smiled and shrugged to her.

"I'll walk him on this dirt path to cool him down," Ray told us watchers. "And then we'll load him and take him off your hands. How is he with trailers?"

"He's OK with trailers if he's not tied, but you might want to use a stud chain on him while you walk him. I do. You can't trust him otherwise."

"Thanks, but I'm more concerned with him trusting me. We'll be okay, and I've got the chain if I need it. We'll be right back, and then I've got another question for you, if you've got the time."

The man nodded yes, he did, and Ray and the horse walked away down a dirt path beside the corrals. They were headed away from where we three sat on a fence near the barn.

Human and horse both looked calm and relaxed, but when they turned around to come back toward the barn, there was a short scuffle as Taz tried to take off toward the barn. When Pa held him back, he made a move to try and bite Pa. Pa said, "quit," in his customary firm 'I-mean-business' tone, and immediately turned the horse back around in the other direction. Again, they were walking away from the barn and where we three sat and observed.

Away they walked together, and after a minute or two, Pa moved Taz in a circle the width of the dirt path. Then they reversed and circled in the other direction. Coming out of the second circle, Pa led Taz back towards the barn, and this time, the horse did not attempt to speed up or make any aggressive moves at Pa.

"Right there," Ruby said to me, "the horse learned he didn't get what he wanted by acting like a butt. He's smart, this Tasmanian Devil horse. He learns quick."

She made the man sitting on the fence with us

chuckle. Then he answered her, but kept watching Pa and the horse.

"Smart, he is. And quick, too. But you've got to pay attention all the damn time when you're working with him. Otherwise he gets the best of you whenever he feels like it. Looks like your Ray Keegan is pretty smart as well, at least with horses he must be."

"Yep. Very smart. But he's not *my* Ray Keegan; he's my boss. And he's her father."

The guy looked at Ruby and smiled. She looked back at him but she didn't smile.

Later I told Pa, "While you were schooling the horse, Ruby was schooling me and the fellow who gave him to us."

Pa did smile; he even laughed when I told him that. He was smiling a lot when we got back to the farm since our new horse had walked right into the trailer and stood untied and munched on hay all the way.

We loaded Taz after Pa asked if a veterinarian had checked him out, and yes, the horse was physically sound. But Pa and the man giving him to us agreed that it was hard to know a horse's history when you bought him at feedlot or kill pen auction. He could have had all kinds of bad treatment and neglect in his past. He could have been sold any number of times and been used in all kinds of ways he wasn't suited to.

It wasn't till the evening of the day we added Taz to our roster of rescued horses that we discovered how monumental of an undertaking this was going to be.

Taz enjoyed his time in the small lot Pa had put him in. He nibbled on bits of grass available there and cleaned up the rest of the trailer hay plus a flake of alfalfa lunch hay Pa gave him. He could see and smell the other horses pastured around him, but he could not have physical contact with any of them. He had plenty of fresh water and room to move around at his free will. He took advantage of all of it, too. So far, so good.

However, as the sun set, we had to bring him into the barn. Pa and Gary had cleared and bedded a box stall for him. It was a frontend stall near the barn doors and had an open space where wheelbarrows were stored on one side, and an empty stall beside it on the other side, but Taz (Ruby insisted 'Taz' was a better name than 'Devil' for the horse) would be directly across the barn from Freckles' stall so he could see and smell another horse. And since the sides of the stalls were topped with strong iron gridwork, Taz could also see across the empty stall to Rufus in his box stall.

All the box stalls have half-doors with open tops so the horses can put their heads out and look around inside the high-ceilinged and wide-isled barn. Pa cautioned all of us to never forget when we were walking past Taz's stall, to every time give his stall some distance in case he tried to bite at passersby. Pa told us he might have to put a stall-guard above Taz's stall door to keep the horse from lunging out at people or other horses going past. Eventually Taz got his stall-guard after Pa decided on his permanent stall, which ended up being the one Pa originally put him in.

But that first evening our supper was delayed while we watched Pa simply trying to take Taz into his stall with his supper hay already in the stall. He got two flakes of alfalfa and a small flake of timothy. We feed mostly timothy and orchard grass with a small flake or two of alfalfa, but at his former home Taz got alfalfa and oat. When Taz got used to grass hays, he'd get fed with the portions reversed, like the other horses.

Pa figured the strong and sturdy horse might try to charge into the stall, and he also knew he couldn't let the animal get away with that. Since Taz also had a tendency to charge at the person feeding him, Pa decided to take him to the hay, rather than the hay to him. Either way could be a challenge.

Pa explained to us that he didn't want to use a stud-chain since it might cause the horse to rear up inside the stall. Even though the barn ceilings are high, that could be dangerous. So, Pa carried, looped around his wrist, a short western style riding crop, sometimes called a quirt, and when he needed to, tapped Taz on the chest with the quirt to get him to back up when he had tried to charge into the stall.

It took four tries to get Taz walking with Pa into his stall, turning calmly, stopping and letting Pa take off his halter and lead-line before he stepped forward and started eating his hay. Pa's mouth was set in a grim line the whole time, except for when he said 'quit' or 'back' or 'good,' but he was patient and calm with the horse the whole time, also.

Gary got restless and couldn't stand watching after the first two tries, and Pa asked him to go to the house and let Dulce know we'd most likely be a little late to supper. Maybe Gary would also be so kind as to help her set the table since Pa wanted Ruby and I to stay and observe the training of Taz. Gary agreed right off; he often stayed and ate supper with us now, mainly because he loves Ma's cooking.

While the three of us watched Taz enjoy his alfalfa, Pa spoke softly to Ruby and me.

"This monkey is going to take time, effort, patience and strategy on our part. He's going to be the second horse turned out in the morning and the next to the last horse brought in at night. After he adjusts to grazing, we're going to put him in the field farthest from the barn, and he'll have a flake of hay already on the ground when we turn him out. But we can't let him rush into pasture any more than we let him rush into his stall. When you start giving the other horses their hay, give him another flake first, right before you feed Lurcher."

"Why make him go second instead of first?" asked Ruby.

"I don't want him alone out in pasture or alone inside the barn. The guy who gave him to us told me this horse has been known to almost kick a stall apart when he was the only horse in the barn. I doubt he can ever be pastured in the same field with another horse, but as long as he can see and smell another horse, but not be able to threaten or bully other horses, I think he might do all right.

"Another thing," Pa continued, "he pulls back. So, don't ever try to tie him. Not even once. If he needs to be contained outside an enclosure, like when I trim his feet or for the vet, someone has to hold him. That someone will be Ruby or me, and nobody else, at least for now. He might ground-tie, but I don't trust him yet."

"Pull back?" I asked Ruby while Pa doublechecked all the barn critters.

"Oh, girl," she said to me. "If you've ever seen the drama of it or dealt with it, you know. Believe me, I've experienced it before and if you have, you hope and pray it never happens again in your presence. Some can be trained out of it, maybe, but with this 'monkey,' as your Pa says, better to not even try."

"But how do we clean his feet or brush him?" I had to ask.

"Don't worry about it; your Pa and I will handle that. Someday, if he behaves better, I'll hold him and you can clean him up when he needs it. Trust me, Agga," (my name is Agnes), "that beaut ain't getting away with shit when I hold him. That's for damn sure."

By the end of Taz's first year with us, that's what we were doing. Ruby would lead him out of his pasture and hold him for me to pick his feet out and occasionally brush him off, wasting no time doing it. If he got ornery, she'd quick, bop him on the shoulder with her fist. Pa had told us to not use our hands or halter or lead rope to discipline a horse since he didn't want the horses to associate everyday means of handling with corrective discipline. But Ruby kept out her fist as an exception and told me that if she stuck her thumb between her fingers when she made a fist, it would feel natural to a horse.

"Feels like another horse using teeth to set the ground rules, you know," she said.

But I objected a little. "Shouldn't you check with Pa?"

"What Ray doesn't know won't give him headaches."

And I never told, so we left it at that.

For a whole year and eight months of Taz, it was good times and rough times interspersed. Then something happened that worked almost like a miracle. Pa bought a new plow horse for the farm so Rufus could relax and enjoy his retirement.

The day Pa trailered Jasper in was a happy, glorious day for all of us. Even Taz. We were all surprised, Ruby and Ma and Gary and me, when a young Norwegian Fjord Horse gelding was backed carefully out of Pa's trailer. He looked all around, breathed in the air, and checked out the other horses in pasture, like he already owned the place. And did he ever.

Small, just under 14 hands, but stout, sturdy, strong and confidant, that Jasper was super cute with a personality to match. And he took to the farm, like the farm took to him, from the minute he arrived.

Ruby said it for the rest of us. "You've heard of love at first sight? Well, this is it, my friends. Meant to be. Just abso-fucking-lutely, meant to be." She glanced at Pa as she walked past him to make over our new horse. "Oh baby, you did good here, Ray. You did good."

Didn't none of us know just what to say about that, but it turned out, she was right.

Seven-year-old Jasper was already acclimated to grazing, but Pa put him in a grazed-down pasture just in case and put hay in with him. Since that field happened to be behind Taz's pasture, we all kept watch on the two horses in case there was any ruckus. Even Ma took a few turns at watch. But both animals ignored each other and ate grass and hay in peace.

Night time would tell the tale. The only stall readily available for Jasper was the empty stall between Rufus and Taz. Ma actually postponed supper so she could join the rest of us observing the 'big moment' when Ruby led the little Fjord pony into his stall. Pa stood on the ready beside the front of Taz's stall.

Almost exactly like in pasture. We could hardly believe it. When Ruby set Jasper free of halter and lead, he walked over to the grid between his and Taz's stalls, and Taz did the same. They sniffed noses and went back to their hay and ate. On Jasper's other side, Rufus took a mouthful of hay, raised his big head and glanced over at our new plowing horse. Jasper glanced back at him, then both returned to their hay.

None of us could be certain, but in time we all relaxed a little. Jasper was pastured next to Taz; they were separated by only one fence, but all went well. Jasper simply wasn't threatened by Taz and they became friends. They would do a little of that 'gelding mouthy' thing over top of their fence; I worried, but Ruby said they were just playing.

"That's the ticket," she told me. "You can't feel threatened by Taz; you just have to be cautious but brave. Kind of like with men. Be as bold as you want but keep an eye on 'em. Don't let them get away with shit. Works for me anyway, girl."

And that's what I really like about Ruby. She treats me like I'm another girl. I don't think Gary realizes I'm a girl, and I don't really think of myself as one either. To Pa and Ma, I'm a kid and farm worker. And Dr. Spelling never pays attention to anyone except Pa and the horses. I sort of feel like I'm a neutral, a thing. Except with Ruby. And the quiet, gentle horses; they come to me. Because I feed them.

Our new farm pony Jasper showed himself to be a

good worker and a character to boot. For a while Ruby and I helped Ma with housework so Ma could lead Jasper while he plowed fields with Pa driving. But he caught on quick and only needed to be led on days when he didn't especially feel like working, but those days were seldom. And he had stamina; he and Pa accomplished more farm work than anybody, especially Gary, expected.

"He's a runt, looks like a kid's pony, Keegan! How can he plow as much as big old Rufus used to? What in blazes made you buy him?"

That was Gary's reaction on seeing Jasper in harness and hitched to the plow the first time. Pa just shrugged his shoulders and smiled before he answered.

"Wait a little. He'll do fine. And he eats less than large draft horses need to. Plus, he gets along with Taz, doesn't he? What more do you need, Gary? After Dulce breaks him in for me, you can guide him till he learns how to go on his own with just me driving. You'll love it. It'll be easy; you can see over top of him since you're taller than he is."

Jasper is like paradise to work with and handle. He's a little mouthy, but he only uses lips, never teeth. Pa discourages hand-feeding anyway, with all the horses; we feed treats like apples or carrots in feed tubs, which Jasper makes excellent use of. After he finishes his snack, he plays with the empty tub, rolls it, flips it, and sometimes carries it or tosses it, using his mouth. He's an all-around personality-plus individual.

He loves to be groomed, scratched, petted and rubbed, loves people, and he likes other critters on the farm. When Jasper's relaxing in his pasture, that dog Persk will sometimes join him if Pa opens the gate, and they play together, each of them pushing Jasper's tether ball around. Looks like soccer. It's hilarious. Jasper will even nuzzle the chickens or barn cats if any are around when he's led out of his stall in the morning.

Up until around three-and-a-half months ago, all was pretty quiet and peaceful around the farm. Pa knew change was coming, but he did not say anything to Ruby, Gary or me, possibly not even to Ma, in case things didn't work out. We three outdoor workers kind of wondered, Ruby out loud to Gary and me, why Pa had us clearing out a stall area in the back of the barn, next to the back doors, but none of us asked Pa.

Then, working with Pa, we put up a new stall, beside Teddy's stall and across from the chicken coop. We only worked on it while Teddy, the other horses, and the chickens were out in pasture. When we finished it, Pa put in bedding and a place for a water container. Strangely, it wasn't Ruby who asked; it was Gary.

"So, we're getting a new rescue horse, right, Keegan?"

Ray Keegan just shook his head, no. And walked out of the barn. That was so maddening to me, I didn't want to call him 'Pa' anymore. That night at supper, Mr. and Mrs. Keegan talked only about how the soybean, spinach, hay and corn crops were doing, and the upcoming apple harvests. Ruby, Gary and I looked at each other like we were being driven crazy. We kind of were.

Ruby couldn't stand it any longer. "What's with the new stall we just built?"

No answer; they kept eating like nothing was said.

"Who's throwing who out of the house?" asked Gary, in his joking way. "And who's sleeping in the stall tonight? You, Keegan? Or the lady of the house?"

Granted, not in the best of taste, but Gary didn't actually mean anything awful by it. But it ended up being awful. Ma got up from the table and, without a word, left our eating area. Pa stood up fast and angry, almost knocking his chair over behind him. He stood, palms down on the table, glaring at each of us in turn, and shook his head. When he spoke, his voice was raspy with aggravation.

"A little respect would be nice for me," he told us, "but for the person who cooks and cleans for you every day, it *should* be mandatory. Why don't you all finish your supper quietly, and go to bed. We've got an early morning ahead of us, and I want you three to be rested and ready to work. I want all the horses out in pasture and fed, well before seven, and all of the stalls cleaned. Dulce will take care of the chickens, Persk and the cats, like she usually does. I'll put fresh water in the new stall. I'm going to bed, too. Goodnight."

"Wait a minute, Keegan!" Gary yelped.

Ruby flinched and I jumped in place in my seat. She had been cleaning up her plate; we all always clean up our food. And I was sitting there frozen, afraid to even lift up my spoon to eat. Gary startled us, all three.

"Why don't you tell us what's going on? Are we androids or something? You tell us what to do and we do it, but you don't tell us why! Does that seem fair to you? What the hell is happening? Don't we have a right to know? What if we do something wrong since we're totally in the dark? Are you going to fire us then, or what?"

"I don't want to jinx anything," Pa muttered under his breath, and left the kitchen in a hurry.

"Fu…," Gary made a sound under his breath, and he and I glanced at each other, both of us puzzled and nervous.

Ruby looked up at us while she kept eating. "Better eat up, so we can do the dishes and go to bed. You heard him, we're early tomorrow. He's got his reasons for not telling, and we'll find out when we find out. Last person finished supper washes, but relax cause I'm having thirds since Mr. and Mrs. left the table."

We boogied that night and also early next morning. At twenty after seven in the morning, Dr. Joel Spelling drove his trailer up to the area near the barn and starter pasture, where we unload the rescued horses. Pa opened the trailer and the doc went in and slowly and carefully led the animal down the ramp, turned her around in a big circle and handed her to Pa.

Were we ever surprised? Pa had not lied. She wasn't a horse. Lizette is a mule. The sweetest, most adorable mule anybody's ever seen.

She's sand-colored, a true dun, with a fuzzy black forelock, a black stripe down her back, and legs with zebra stripes on the knees, and a slightly mealy muzzle with black on the end of her nose. Her big, tall ears are lined with black but have dun-shaded fur along the insides. At first sight, to my mind, she was the perfect size: around 14.2 hands, and the ideal weight with short, muscled legs, and what looked like a 'mile-wide' chest. Her mane was hogged, shaved off almost to her skin, but her tail, although kind of short, looked like a full horse tail at the bottom.

Lizette's large dark eyes had the kindest, smartest expression I'd ever seen on anybody or anything.

Her story was a true horror show. But with a partway happy ending. Involving no purposeful human cruelty or neglect, only panicked rider judgment and unforeseen extreme bad luck, it was a tragic accident.

Dr. Spelling had told Pa the story months ago, soon after it happened, and Pa told Ma a few weeks ago and then the rest of us on the morning we met Lizette. After Pa put her in the 'starter' pasture, next to the one Teddy was in, he described the basics of how that darling riding mule had been severely injured.

Three experienced trail riders, two of them riding solid trail-tested mounts, the other training a newly purchased horse, were traveling up a mountain on a very narrow, winding trail. On one side of the trail was a steep and rocky slope down into a ravine, on the opposite side, the high mountain wall. The portion of the trail they were on when the accident happened accommodated only single file; trying to pass or turn around on it could be extremely dangerous.

As common sense dictated, the trio had the inexperienced horse in the middle, with Lizette leading and a calm, seasoned trail pony bringing up the rear.

All three riders had travelled this same trail before without incident, and the same for Lizette and the last horse in line. Even though parts of the trail were pretty dicey for beginners, the new horse had been touted as an excellent trail pony, and normally they should have had a cool trail ride with outstanding views.

But well over half way up, and at an extremely narrow portion of trail that curved outward and up, a very loud, jarring, metallic sound echoed out from above and behind the trio. It was sudden, with an unseen origin, and repeated several times in quick succession.

Lizette continued to walk steadily but calmly forward, and the last horse stopped and stood, but the horse in the middle spooked at the sound and jumped, then tried to bolt. His startled rider was unseated, and unable to settle his panicked mount, or right himself in the saddle, he fell off onto the trail.

Trembling, the frightened animal stopped short of running over the edge of the trail or running into Lizette in front of him. His rider, who was unhurt, stood up and stepped quietly and slowly toward him, speaking softly to him, but the terrifying sound happened again, this time louder and longer, and his horse leaped forward on the trail toward Lizette.

The mule, continuing to walk safely up the trail, was pulled to a sudden stop by her owner and rider who, turning around in his saddle in an attempt to catch and stop the scared horse, hit his head on the rocky side of the mountain. He was not wearing a riding helmet. Stunned a little, he kept a hard hold on Lizette's reins, and at the same time reached out with his other hand and grabbed the reins of the horse running up on Lizette.

Several things happened at once. One of the riderless horse's hind feet exceeded the outside edge of the trail, and he began to slide back and down. In his desperate scramble to regain his footing, one of the gelding's front hooves clipped one of the mule's hind legs, right above her fetlock area.

Lizette's rider let go of her reins, allowing her to step forward out of the way of the struggling horse, but too late. When she tentatively put weight on the injured leg, the pain caused her to stop quickly and hold the leg up with her hoof propped on its toe. She then stood still on the trail.

The panicked gelding slid over the edge of the trail and

fell down the mountain. Lizette's rider, still holding the gelding's reins, went with him for a few feet, then was able to let go. He did not land under the horse, but he did land headfirst on a jagged rock and was knocked unconscious. The horse somersaulted down into the ravine.

The third rider in line put his reins, held in one hand, down against his horse's neck, signaling a standstill stay for the horse. With his other hand, he got his cell phone out of a jeans pocket, clicked it on, and dialed 9-1-1. He kept his voice calm, steady and clear as he told about the accident and location, and mentioned the emergency services he felt might be needed. He was correct about everything he asked for. One person and two animals had to be air lifted out.

Amazingly enough, all six survived that ill-fated trail ride, partly due to the level head of the third rider and the steady reliability of his Mustang horse. Plus, incredible intelligence and survival instinct on the part of Lizette the mule, combined with the skill, dedication and fast response of the rescuers.

The rider who fell off slid down the mountain very slowly and cautiously. He first checked on Lizette's owner who was unconscious, then moved down into the ravine, speaking reassuringly to his horse, standing on narrow flat ground and trembling. The saddle had come off during the fall, but the gelding was still wearing his bridle, short one rein. Holding the rein his owner ran a gentle hand all over the horse. The horse's muscles were bruised and sore but his owner found no extreme pain or heat anywhere on the horse, who would make a full recovery but never again be ridden on an exceedingly narrow trail, and would eventually be de-sensitized to sudden, loud noises.

Lizette and her owner both sustained serious injuries. The mule's cannon bone had received a hairline fracture. She was flown to a specialized veterinary clinic equipped to handle large animals. There, she went through many months of treatment aimed at saving her life. Although Lizette was a supremely cooperative patient, her injury was difficult to treat, and demanded an excruciatingly long and meticulous recovery.

Her owner's injury was worse. Pa told us that the poor man suffered a serious head injury from which he would never fully recover. But he could live with it. However, his life changed drastically. His occupation before the accident had paid exceptionally well; plus, he had insurance covering his medical expenses. When he learned while in hospital of Lizette's injury and treatment, which was being paid for by the other two riders, he paid for the remainder of her extended recovery expenses. However, when he got out of the hospital, he was unable to return to his previous job.

His new part-time job paid a lot less, and even though he had assistance supporting himself, he could no longer afford to take care of his beloved mule. Dr. Spelling had been treating Lizette at the recovery clinic, so he offered her owner the possibility of giving her to a rescue retirement home on the Espinosa farm, and visiting her there whenever he could.

That's how we came to know that darling mule.

Her story was hard to hear; it made me recall a moment in an emergency room with 'Her' from the anger house. I was sitting on one of those exam tables and my head ached really bad. I heard a doctor or nurse, I didn't know which, say something to Her about 'these kinds of head injuries.' She said back, that I fell down the stairs, and I knew she was lying. I had a flash of memory and it showed me Her, holding my arms tight while she banged my head against one of the steps. I don't remember what happened before or next, but I remember I was only nine years old.

Anyway, Lizette was a breeze to know and care for. In many ways, she kind of rescued us. After a couple of weeks on our farm, Pa put her in pasture with Teddy, and what a fabulous combo! They were 'together pals' like Freckles and Powder had been, just meant for each other.

Since Pa and Dr. Spelling worry about Teddy foundering again, he can't be turned out in pasture with lots and lots of grass; he has to be in a field with enough grass to browse on, but not enough to really pig out with. Being a mule, Lizette doesn't need to eat as much as the horses; she stays nice and round and happy with her hay, some sporadic grazing, and tub-fed treats like apples, carrots or pears. Except for Jasper, we don't usually feed much grain, or not at all; these animals are not working.

Teddy and Lizette are the right size for each other and they are both slow movers, too. Teddy's withers are only one inch higher than Lizette's, and they will groom each other, scratching each other's neck, out in pasture.

Both of them also get along well with the three pasture-mates turned out beside them: Rufus, Mira, and Freckles. These five sweeties are the group Gary and I usually lead, out to pasture in the morning and back to the barn after it gets dark outside. Pa takes Jasper, and Ruby takes Taz, Lurcher and Rainey, but we get the easies.

Except Gary didn't want to lead Lizette at first. He told Pa he was afraid of her.

"What?" Pa asked him. "That sweet little mule? She doesn't do anything naughty. Why are you afraid?"

Gary got defensive. "It's not anything she does. It's the look in her eyes. She knows everything I'm thinking."

Pa had to laugh. "Well, I guess knowing what *you're* thinking could be pretty scary. Better steer clear of her. Aggie can handle her."

"Yeah," I said, "I'm never thinking anything. There's nothing for her to do with that."

That made Pa laugh again. But Gary put Lizette's halter on her and led her out of the barn, speaking to her as they passed by me and Pa.

"Let's get you out of the range of these idiots. Aren't you glad you're so much smarter than they are?"

Anybody could tell by looking at her eyes, Lizette was thinking she was glad.

****

Two months after Lizette arrived with us was the time for checkups and vaccines for our equines. Lizette already had her shots before she left the recovery clinic, but Dr. Spelling wanted to look her over anyway while he was at our farm. Pa would work it so eventually Lizette's timing was the same as the horses.' He always did that with all the newcomers, if they were with us long enough.

While Dr. Spelling was giving Taz his vaccines with Ruby holding him, he was telling Pa something he forgot to say about Lizette's terrible trail ride accident. He said that the third rider, the one with the mustang, waited until Lizette was safely air lifted off the mountain and then rode the rest of the way up the trail.

At the top, in a large flat campground area, he spoke with two senior adults and their grandson who were all preparing to leave their campsite. He dismounted and gave his horse a well-deserved break and grazing time; then he asked the family if they had heard loud banging sounds earlier. The grandson smiled and said that was him, banging on a tin pot with a metal serving spoon to wake up his grandparents because he was hungry for breakfast. The young man added that he had to bang on the pan two separate times to get them moving because it was early and they were 'getting too old' to go camping. His grandfather objected but his grandmother just giggled at that.

The trail rider chuckled with the family and bid them good day, then remounted and rode down the mountain via the service road trail on the mountain's other side. This trail was wide and with gentle switchbacks, plus much of it was shaded by trees on both sides. The three riders had opted to take the more difficult and strenuous trail up in the early, cool morning, and ride the shaded, easy trail down when the full sun was in evidence. When the man and his trail pony got back to their three-horse trailer, alone, he made a promise with himself to only use the easy trail, up and down, from that day on. He knew he would keep that promise.

Ruby left to put Taz back in his pasture, and I stepped up with Rainey for the vet to treat her next. Rainey is always well behaved, even around veterinarians, so Dr. Spelling was able to ask Pa a quick question.

"Didn't you tell me you learned about horses and how to ride in a program on the inside?"

I thought his question made no sense at all, but Pa answered.

"That's right. Horses saved me."

"Now, you save them," commented Dr. Spelling.

Pa smiled and said, "Some of them. And most of that's *your* fault, Joel."

They were laughing together, and since Rainey had got her exam and vaccines, I was letting her graze nearby. I was hoping they might say more, so I could interpret everything they were talking about, but they only seemed inclined to whisper to each other and chuckle while Pa checked the next horse's chart and Dr. Spelling got vaccines and wormer ready.

Then Ruby was on her way back with Lurcher, and Pa and Dr. Spelling stopped talking. Knowing I should bring Freckles over to see the vet next, I led Rainey back toward her pasture.

Having Dr. Spelling on the property is always an interesting sort of arrangement, and not just regarding shuffling the horses back and forth, either. It's like a complicated dance among the people, too.

See, people, pretty much everybody, like to look at Ray Keegan. He's very handsome, and yet it's more than that. He has something that makes Ma, and for sure Ruby, plus townspeople when we're in town, and even, in a different sort of way, Gary and me, and especially Dr. Spelling, want to watch him, listen to him, kind of take him all in. All of the time.

All kinds of animals are attentive to him also. Maybe that's part of what makes him so good with horses.

Dr. Spelling makes a nice appearance; he's very smooth, and clean and healthy looking. I guess you could say he's cute. Ruby sure thinks so. The first time she met him; she was super friendly to him. She kept chatting and giggling and smiling at him. To no avail, whatsoever. I could have told her; he only pays attention to my Pa.

Sure, the vet is professional and minds what he's doing. He's very kind, patient, gentle and caring with all the horses and the mule. Dr. Spelling loves animals and it shows. As far as people go, he loves Ray Keegan. From what I've seen, only Ray Keegan. When Dr. Spelling hasn't got a horse in front of him, or when he's not working with his meds or writing up his bill, he's watching Ray and listening to him or talking to him.

To be fair, Dr. Spelling is a little friendly with Ma, nodding to her and smiling, and he's polite to the rest of us, me, Gary and even Ruby. But, like Ruby told me once, she wants more than that. And, like she admitted to me later, she is not going to get more.

Ruby also told me, but I did not want to hear it, that the main reason she flirted with Dr. Spelling is that she knows she can't flirt with Ray. Cause Ray is married. Otherwise, Ray Keegan would be the man for her. This was not a surprise to me, but it still made me a little mad at her. Sometimes I don't understand Ruby, even though she lives in the room beside mine.

Sometimes I wish she'd keep her opinions to herself.

I understand why she thinks my Pa is handsome; I see it, like everybody else does. What I don't get is why Joel Spelling is her second choice. I happen to think that Gary Pepper is way cuter and way prettier than Dr. Spelling. But I don't tell Ruby that. Or anyone else.

Seems like Gary and Ruby have what you might call a tentative relationship. When Ruby first appeared for work on our farm, Gary was super enthralled with her. In her own wild and strong way, she's beautiful, and most men look at her with delight in their eyes. Women mostly distrust her, I think, maybe because of the delight on the part of the men. Anyway, Gary made a fool of himself over her, kind of fawning over her and taking any chance he could get to talk with her.

Ruby did not only ignore him; after a week or so of his puppy-dog eyes and silly remarks, she told him off.

"Look," she said to him, "we have to work together here on the farm. You have to quit it with this dumbass notion you have of trying to flirt with me and thinking it's going to go anywhere. It's not. You have zero chance of succeeding with any malarkey you think you want with me. Sorry to be rude, but that's the way it is. I do not hanker to make hay with little boys. I make my living doing physical labor on farms, and that's what I'm here to do. And that's the only thing I'm here for, as far as you're concerned. Are we clear?"

Pa was a distance out of hearing range when she said that to Gary, but I was right there with the two of them. My mouth must have dropped open, I was so surprised by her words, but Gary nodded yes to her. She wasn't looking at him. Ruby stopped pitchforking horse poops into a wheelbarrow and glared at Gary.

"I didn't hear your answer, Gary. Are we clear?"

"Yes, Ma'am," Gary said quickly.

"Good," was Ruby's retort to him. "Let's get this pasture cleaned up. Ray is working circles around us."

After that day, Ruby pretty much treated Gary the same as before, only gradually she worked more with Pa while Gary and I worked together. Gary, however, kept a distance from her whenever he could, and for about a month, he did not have much to say to her. He didn't seem to have much to say to any of us.

I was worried. Ruby talked a blue streak, like she did from the beginning, but Gary kept quiet, when he used to chime in from time to time. One day when Pa and I were cleaning stalls next to each other, and Ruby and Gary were in the back of the barn across the aisle from each other, and Ruby was chatting away but Gary wouldn't even look at her, I looked my upset into Pa's face and he knew what I meant.

"Let them work it out for themselves, Aggie. They'll be all right soon enough. Let's you and I hope I don't need to step in. But I don't think so; I think time will fix it. We'll just wait a little bit longer." He said that really soft so they wouldn't hear him.

And Pa was right. Little by little, Ruby and Gary started talking to each other again, and everyone was back to being themselves. We were a team again.

But one thing I noticed, Ruby had hurt Gary and he was a little afraid of her. They were friends again, and I could tell he still liked to look at her when she wasn't paying attention to him, but he also held a little something back. Until he didn't.

One day when Pa took the three of us into town with him, Ruby and I were walking past the little drugstore with magazines in a rack in the front. We saw Gary in there looking through movie magazines. Ruby couldn't resist teasing him.

"Hey, Gary," she called in to him. "Find any great looking gals you like in there? Any guys? I like to look at both, you know. Maybe more than look."

Ruby laughed, Gary stared open-mouthed at her, and I giggled over both of them. Gary shook his head at Ruby and spoke up so she could hear him from outside the drugstore, but the door was open so she could hear anyway.

"I hope Ray Keegan knows he hired a wild, wild female when he hired you, Ruby!"

Now she shook her head at Gary. "Let me tell you, son. Ray Keegan is one person I know that's not afraid of wild. Not at all."

Ruby walked on past the drugstore while Gary and I stared at each other. His mouth was open a little and he moved his head from side to side slowly. Then he muttered, almost as though talking to himself.

"What a surprise. Well, I know him a lot better than you do, and Ray Keegan is not afraid of much of anything. Why would he be? He married Dulce Espinosa, and in my book, that overshadows 'wild' any day of the week."

He may have been speaking his thoughts out loud to himself only, but I was glad I heard him. When I thought back about it, I really liked what he said.

****

But it was my Pa who made my other favorite statement when we were in town on another day.

Mrs. Holt was speaking with Pa while Ruby and I carried bundles of goods purchased at the general store to our pickup truck. Pa had already deposited most of what we bought in the truck bed and he was socializing with Mrs. Holt, wife of the store owner, and town gossip, know-it-all and busybody. Well, that's just my opinion; sometimes I don't much care for her.

As I stepped down off the boarded walkway in front of the store and other shops, I heard Mrs. Holt use the expression 'heavyset,' and a course I knew she was referring to me. I hate that word and it upsets me every time I hear it.

But my Pa told her. "She's a healthy girl and a good worker. Both my girls are. I couldn't replace them with three men."

****

The barn on the Espinosa farm is traditional, only much bigger than most. It's painted red but faded a bit these days, and stands very tall with double-doors on both ends. And the barn is situated on the property to get good air flow throughout, and on higher ground so it drains well. Plus, it's pretty close to the farmhouse.

What's unusual about the property is the house itself. That's a single-story rectangular adobe building with a fairly large open courtyard in the center. The rooms are built around the courtyard, almost all of them with doors opening into the partly roofed, partly screened-in walkway-lined grassy center that contains a smallish tree and a good-sized fountain. The house's front door faces Sugarhill Road where it curves around past our farm. The back door opens to a dirt path running around the back of Ma's fenced in garden.

Exiting out either door will give you a fairly short walk to the barn.

With the front door opening into a huge living room that stretches across the whole front of the home, and the large eat-in kitchen and pantry, washroom with sink, washing and drying machines, two clotheslines, plus a small mudroom, all in the back, the four bedrooms and two bathrooms line both sides of the house along the length of the courtyard. No dining room needed.

There is a coat closet in front of a linen closet, then a big bathroom between the living room and the primary bedroom that belongs to Ma and Pa. Across the courtyard is a normal size bathroom, then my room, then Ruby's, and last, a bedroom Gary uses sometimes. Lately, he uses it more often. All the bedrooms have closets; in the primary, the closet is the whole length of one wall. The other closets are small, but then the other bedrooms are also small.

Ruby told me that with this house being as old as it is (Ma's great grandfather built it), she's surprised that there are any closets at all. Just armoires instead. She had to spell that for me and explain it was like a furniture chest of drawers except taller and you could hang clothes inside it, but I still can't imagine what it looks like.

The windows to the outside of our adobe house aren't real big, but almost all of the rooms have doors to the edges of the open air courtyard; plus, they have screen doors in front of the solid doors, so you can prop the inside door open and fresh air from the courtyard comes into your room. I love that, especially when there is cool air outside at night and early in the morning to offset the sun's heat during the day.

Pa had to put a screened dome over top of the courtyard though, because Ma has an indoor cat now, and even though that dog Persk stays in the house at night, hawks have been seen around our area.

Ma's housecat is named Anita, and most of our current barn cats were kittens from her litters over the years before she got surgery and moved indoors. Ma told me there's been a feral tomcat roaming around here for over a decade. Anita herself was discovered long ago, pregnant at the time and wandering along outside our fences and beside Sugarhill Road. Somebody must have dropped her out of a car.

On an indoor workday I had, due to being plagued by my miserable 'visitor,' Ma told me about how we found Anita and she found us. I couldn't stand the idea of a living creature being tossed out of a car.

"How can people be so cruel?" I asked Ma.

Ma said, "I dunno. History, maybe."

"History? Like that boring class in school where I had to memorize all those past dates?"

"No," Ma answered. "Like their own personal history."

"Like their past makes them mean?"

"Kind of," said Ma. "But not everybody with a hard past is mean. And not everyone with a good past is happy."

I didn't say anything more just then, and we stopped talking for a bit. I just watched Anita chase and jump and bat at a toy mouse on a cord attached to a wand that Ma held and swung back and forth and around.

A wand. Now, I had to ask.

"Wand. That's like magic, isn't it?"

Ma said, "It *is* magic. I believe all cats have magic inside their minds, Aggie."

That was one time I felt really and truly close to Ma, sitting there in the courtyard grass with the sun and fresh air all around. And watching Ma play with Anita, just like she and the old cat were little girls again. It wasn't the first time the farm called to me, but it may have been the first time I listened.

Between the barn area and the back of the house lies Ma's huge, partly treelined and fully fenced garden. Pa put deer fencing around the small grassy plot in front and behind that, the entire garden. The chickenyard and garden fencing is high and even includes screen roofing to allow sun, fresh air and rain in, but keep wild critters and hawks and owls out.

The chickens are allowed in the garden during the day but restricted by bird netting over some areas of the garden, like the majority of Ma's blueberry patch and part of the larger tomato and zucchini vines. A small section of tomato and zucchini vines spill over into the grassy area fronting the garden so Ma's chickens and Hombre the rooster can enjoy their favorite veggies without depriving us humans.

The main garden is like a massive work of art.

Around the outer edges on both sides, fig and persimmon trees provide a partial canopy for dwarf apple (fuji and yellow delicious), Bartlett pear, and peach trees, scattered around and through parts of the garden. All the trees also serve as cover for foraging chickens, and some as arbors for climbing tomato vines.

Trailing rosemary herb plants circle the garden center, which gets full sun and is interspersed with zucchini, spinach, carrots, bronze fennel, lavender, nasturtium (with edible leaves and yellow, orange and red flowers, also edible), parsley, catmint, and alpine strawberries, in addition to the patch of southern highbush blueberry bushes, mostly netted over to make them inaccessible to chickens. Otherwise, farm humans could never eat or sell blueberries.

Dirt paths also meander through the garden. These allow Ma to tend the trees, bushes, plants and flowers, and offer occasional dust baths to the chickens and rooster, although they also have the grassy dirt area fenced off in front of the garden.

Gary once called the chickenyard in front of Ma's garden the 'vestibule,' which he insisted was what you called a church's foyer. Maybe it is; us residents of the Espinosa farm don't go to church. I guess the Peppers do, cause Gary's never here on our farm on Sunday mornings. Evidently vestibule fits since the garden is like church to Ma and the chickens.

When Gary said his name for the chicken yard, I

looked at Pa right away. He knew why, too. Pa and I like words and we like to learn new ones. Later, when we were back in the house in the evening, Pa told me how to spell vestibule so I could add it to my running list of words we like. I keep the list with my diary in my room along with my books. Pa and I like to read as well, and sometimes he brings books home, as presents for me.

One time, Ruby came into my room to talk and she saw my books and diary with the word list in it. She tapped the word list and asked what it was. I handed it to her to look at, and told her how Pa and I like to collect words. As she handed it back to me, Ruby pointed to the word 'armoire' on the list, and smiled at me. She did not pick up my diary, just looked at it and then at me with a 'my-my' kind of expression. I said nothing. After that, nosy as she is, she knelt down on the tile floor and went through my books, touching each one as she went.

I don't have a regular bookcase, just a board sitting on top of two separated short stacks of three bricks, each. The books sit on top of the board and are held up with heavy piggybank bookends against the first and last book. There are enough books to almost cover the board, but I haven't read that many of them – I'm a slow reader. Besides, Pa told me to wait a little while before I read at least four them, the last four, from left to right. That's because he said those have some serious cruelty and sadness in them, but they were great books.

My books, left to right, are: "Moby Dick" by Herman Melville; "The No. 1 Ladies' Detective Agency" by Alexander McCall Smith ; "All Creatures Great And Small" by James Herriot; "The Jungle Book" by Rudyard Kipling, "Seabiscuit" by Laura Hillenbrand; "Jane Eyre" by Charlotte Bronte; "Wuthering Heights" by Emily Bronte; "A Little Yellow Dog" by Walter Mosley; "Felicia's Journey" by William Trevor; "Room" by Emma Donoghue; and "City of Bones" by Michael Connelly.

"You've got books," said Ruby. "I used to read when I was young, like you. Not much anymore though. The only book of yours I've read is the one by Michael Connelly. If you want to read about L. A., read him."

"City of Bones. Pa told me that's one of his favorite books. Also books by Walter Mosley. I haven't read those yet, though."

"What's your favorite?"

"The No. 1 Ladies' Detective Agency," I smiled big when I said this. "That book makes me happy every time I think about it. After I've read the others, I want to read it again."

Ruby studied my book titles for a moment.

"Where'd you get all these books?" she asked.

"Pa," I said.

"How did your Pa know what books to give you?" was her next question.

"He read some of them. And he asked two of my teachers, and Mrs. Holt from the store, and Viola in town, and that lady that works at the feed store sometimes. Dr. Spelling read 'Room' and brought it here for Pa to give to me."

I kind of hoped she was through with questions. But no.

"Didn't your Ma give you any books?"

"Ma doesn't like to read. She likes to sew, and knit, and look at magazines, mostly for recipes, and sing, and play with Anita and the chickens, and fix things."

"Your ma sings?"

"You should hear her. Her voice is so pretty. She plays guitar, too. We used to listen to her music in the living room, after we had supper. I don't know why we quit."

"Huh. You are a never-ending revelation, girl," Ruby said before she left my room.

I wondered if Ruby was the reason Ma stopped singing. And if she was, why.

****

The Espinosa farmland covers over fifty acres, but Pa

said it's considered a small farm. I did not understand that, but Gary told me the size of a farm is determined by how much money it makes. Gary also said that it's so hard for family farms to make money, it's next to impossible for them to be classified as large.

Every so often Pa rotates the horse pastures so grass can be planted in the fields not in use. He rotates the crops also; one planting season, a field might have soybeans, the next season, corn. Once in awhile he might grow grass in a field that had crops in before, and then use that as horse pasture.

Our fields to the north of the barn and farmhouse area are mostly flat and used for row crops, like soybeans, baby spinach or corn, to grow timothy and alfalfa hay, and as pasture. The horse fields are closer to the barn, and the row crops and hay farther out. Pa has divided a few of the larger fields in half or smaller to make extra pasture space since we have more rescued animals and some, like Taz, need separate pastures all to themselves.

To the northeast and east, our land rises gradually, toward the mountain range. That back acreage is where the apple orchards are, plus we grow orchard grass hay back there.

Sometimes the fields on the western end of Sugarhill, way out where the road branches out from the highway, are planted with corn, soybeans, baby spinach or wheat. But Pa never puts animals out there close to the highway. There are fences, good fences, all around and through the farm, but Pa and Ruby both say that you never can trust people. People passing by, going north on the highway, could throw something nasty into those fields. Plus, they don't have very many trees in them, and zero manmade shelters.

Espinosa farmland lies between the mountains and the ocean; there are some beachside properties on the ocean side of the highway. Farmland along this stretch has good rich soil for crops, and these days, does not come cheap. But Ma's great grandfather bought our land a long, long time ago, so he got a good deal, at least according to what Gary told me.

Gary also said that the Espinosa's did things the old way. Like plowing using horses instead of tractors. And keeping chickens to help with the garden. Gary insisted that our kind of chickens, Cochins, really aren't good 'laying' chickens and they can be 'broody.' They roost, then nest and sit on their eggs, and when eggs hatch, the hens protect the peeps; they are naturally good moms. So, we never have eggs to sell, only eggs we eat or give to neighbors; and we don't sell the chickens for meat either, just give some to neighboring farms when people want them as pets and/or gardeners.

Ma always tries to find good homes for the chicks when we have too many to keep them. Gary says this is kind of crazy and counterproductive (I wrote that word down after). Pa was with Gary and me when this conversation was happening, and he gave Gary a silent shut-up glance, like he sometimes does. But

Gary doesn't often shut up after he gets going.

Gary went on, "Your Ma could make some money selling chicks to other farmers to raise for meat. Cochins are big; chicken farmers would pay, I think. I bet some farmers Dulce gave chickens to, will either sell them or use them to raise chickens for food to make money."

Pa made serious eye to eye contact with Gary.

"Possibly. But don't you dare tell Dulce that. She loves those chickens, every single one. It would break her heart to hear that, son."

"Yeah, I know," said Gary. "She thinks of them as her grandchildren. But I do NOT think of you as my father."

Pa and I burst into laughter. We couldn't stop. Gary giggled at himself. Many times, he's funny even when he doesn't try to be.

Once, after a visit from Dr. Spelling, Gary got going about how the vet was so fussy, and too picky and clean, to the point of being kind of prissy. I could tell Pa was getting aggravated, and wished Gary would stop talking, but it was as though he couldn't stop.

"I don't know what it is with that guy! It's like everything has to be so completely, prettily perfect all the time. Kind of like he's a schoolmarm, or something!"

Pa had had it. He hollered at Gary, "That's enough!

"Sometimes I don't know *how* I put up with your ignorant goings on!"

Defensive as usual, Gary looked at him and shouted back, "I don't know WHY you put up with them!"

We, Pa and Ruby and I, just stared at Gary for a minute. Then we all cracked up. Pa laughed so hard, he got red in the face. Gary stood there with a silly grin plastered on, but it was obvious, he didn't know what was funny. Actually, I'm not sure the rest of us completely knew either. It was like, that he would say that himself; it just struck us funny that way, I guess.

Ma really does tend to coddle, as well as cuddle, her chickens. Hombre, the red rooster, also. She pays attention to them so she knows them as individuals and their behaviors. She's got Lulubelle, Rosetta, Lupita, Nancy Beth, Pearl, Marla, Posey, Darlene, Vera, Chiquita, Sylvia, and Hortense. Plus, Dabney, who is kind of a rooster, and kind of not. And during the spring and summer, some of the hens have peeps on the ground, or they're sitting on hopefully fertilized eggs in their nest box. Hopefully, because when they sit on eggs that won't hatch, it's sad. Doesn't happen often though.

When the mother hens are ready to take their peeps out of the barn in the mornings, Ma confines them, the hens and their chicks, to the chickenyard in front. She doesn't let them go back into the garden. That's because sometimes in the past, a little chick or two would get lost out in the garden, and then everybody would get upset and very, very loud. These days Ma won't let the youngsters into the garden until they're close to full size chickens.

We look to gather eggs two times each morning. Early, but after the horses and mule are all out in pasture and barn doors at both ends are open, we scatter the chickenfeed around the 'vestibule' and open up the chickencoop inside the barn. Hombre and Dabney are almost always the first ones out of the barn and into their yard. Dabney starts pecking for food, but Hombre stands near the largest pile of food and calls to the hens to come get their breakfast. He lets them eat first. What a gentleman!

After the hens leave the coop to join Hombre and Dabney in the chickenyard, we gather any eggs that don't have hens sitting on them. Then we scatter some chickenfeed in the front of the coop. If nesting hens leave their boxes, we take some of the eggs from their nests, but we leave one or two for them to sit on.

If hens don't leave their eggs during the early feeding, we put more feed down in the coop and check for eggs again, later in the morning. But during the second check also, we don't take all of a nesting hen's eggs away unless we know they won't hatch.

Pearl is a new and unique little pullet. She's a silver-laced frizzle Cochin and was a gift to Ma from another farm. Frizzle feathers curl outward instead of lying flat. She's extra cuddly but also needs extra attention to her fluffed-out feathers. Sometimes Ma takes her inside the house to groom her. She looks so soft and fluffy, like a 'lap chicken' or a living feather duster. Pearl is a young hen and hasn't laid any eggs yet. Ma says it will be interesting if she takes to Hombre; most hens do. If Pearl has chicks, some may be frizzles.

But Ma told me, if there are any live male frizzle chicks, male chicks are called cockerels, we should probably give them away or neuter them (like Dabney was, even though he's not a frizzle). That's because a frizzle to frizzle cross could produce a chick with a lot of health problems. She said if we had any silkie roosters, which we don't, a part frizzle, part silkie chick could be called a 'sizzle,' and that would be okay.

I loved that so much, I added the words 'sizzle chick' to my word list and told Pa about it.

He laughed and said, "So if we had a silkie cock to mate with Pearl, we could look forward to sizzling?"

"We maybe could," I answered. "But it would still be up to Pearl, and we don't have a silkie boy anyway."

That was too silly, and I was glad Ma didn't hear us, kind of trash talking about her chickens.

Our chicken coop is big, and one structure in it has two roosting perches, one low and the other a little higher and positioned farther back than the low perch, in the long, wide rectangular box. There is also a separate row of nesting boxes, equipped with nesting material, for the hens.

We, Ma and me, spot clean the chicken coop every morning and in the chickenyard and garden every late afternoon. We also do a good cleaning weekly and a mammoth clean-out of the coop every three months. Some of what we clean up goes into composting for the garden. Ma also crushes egg shells for composting, helping to prove chickens can be good for gardens. Also, they eat bugs that are detrimental to veggies, fruits and flowers, plus they stir things up when they scratch the dirt. Can be good, unless they stir up too much. But that's Ruby's job. Or Gary's part-time hobby.

Persk, that oddball dog, has a job, too. Actually, a lot of jobs; Pa says he needs to have jobs. In addition to patrolling inside the house at night, he makes the rounds to guard the chicken coop and yard and garden, all during the day. At least a couple of passes in the morning, and a couple more during the late afternoon and evening. Along with Hombre, Persk kind of supervises getting the chickens back into the coop inside the barn before we bring the horses and mule in.

He's a good worker, Persk is. And he never chases chickens, chicks, cats or equines. He knows better. Persk will chase rats or mice though, and catch any the cats miss if he sees them. When that happens, it's a quick kill; he shakes them and they're gone. He won't eat them either. Like some of our barn cats, he presents his kills to one of us, usually Ma or Pa, and the humans put them in a plastic bag in the trash.

They can't be buried because Persk might find them and dig them up. He's got a pretty good nose.

Many times, if it's cool before we eat supper, and if Persk hasn't worked too hard during the day, Pa will play with him outside, close to the front of the house. They both really enjoy this; Pa throws a ball and Persk chases it. When he gets the ball, he shakes it like he caught a rat, and sometimes he brings it right back to Pa, but other times, he throws it himself, for himself. That makes Pa laugh a lot, and the dog looks like he's laughing, too.

Kind of funny looking, Persk is medium sized but very robust, active, healthy and strong. Pa said he thinks our mongrel may be part Pit Bull and part Pug, and part something else, not sure what. Jack Russell, maybe? Or some kind of Heeler? He's got fairly short hair, luckily, and his coat is tan with white areas but not spots. He has big, black, laughing eyes, darkly lined standup pointy ears, a black button nose and a black-lined mouth. His muzzle is rounded on the end and not pushed in like a Pug's but a little shorter than a Pit's and not quite as wide.

Persk almost looks like a dun dog, but never a dumb dog. One glance can tell you he's as smart as bejesus. Strange, but clever. If you ask me, he makes book on Ruby and Gary calling him a mutt, and he doesn't like it. He kind of favors Pa and Ma and me; when one of us makes over him, he yips with delight, and it's cute.

But I don't think he knows that I call him a mutt behind

his back. Nobody told him, and I hope it stays that way since once in a while, I let him into my room at night and he sleeps on the end of my bed. I love that. Makes me feel safe when I know he's there.

With his dun colored coat, Persk bizarrely resembles the dog version of Jasper or Lizette. If you see all three of them together, they might be a matched set – dog and pony and mule. They get along with each other, too. He and Jasper play together and Lizette puts her head down to the dog's level so he can gently pull on one of her ears. I think she likes it from Persk, just like she likes it when one of us does that, but we do it differently and with hands, not lips.

Our daytime barn dog is also friendly with our full-time barn cats. We've got: long-haired orange tabby male Sandy; brown, black and white tabby brothers, Baxter, long-haired, and Dexter, short-hair; white and black Delilah; white and black Mazeppa, who's younger and fluffier than Delilah; and little black and white Minxi, who is short-haired, feisty, and, along with Mazeppa and Dexter, one of the best mousers of the bunch.

Funny, how the three tabbies are all males and the three black-and-whites are all females. All of the current barn cats have had their surgeries and vaccines at the pet clinic in town. Likewise, Anita the housecat and Persk the dog.

Sandy, Baxter, and Mazeppa hang out in the big barn at night, while Minxi and Delilah usually stay in the separate building Pa built to house the hay and feed.

Dexter alternates at will; he's a rover. During the days, in good weather, with the doors to both buildings open, all barn cats can wander as they please.

At night, we feed inside the barn and the hay shed, partly so our cats can stay safe from night critters, and partly so they're in place to catch any rats or mice that come out after dark. Mornings, we also feed the cats inside whichever structure we find them in. They have litter trays in both buildings and we clean those twice a day, same with Anita's trays in the house.

****

From sunup to sundown, we're always busy on the farm.

During spring, summer and early fall, we eat a big breakfast while it's still dark outside, and we work all the way through to dusk with short water breaks, taking in or letting out, and maybe a light lunch of apples or nuts somewhere between noon and two o'clock. Then, after it's dark out, we wash up, have a huge supper, relax for an hour or more, while Ray checks the main barn and hay barn critters, and we all go to bed early, by nine, nine-thirty, latest.

Ruby says this is why she does farm work, so she doesn't have time or energy to be naughty. I wonder about that. She sure can talk naughty at times.

One time, out in a field where we were checking the corn crop, Ruby asked Pa a question that I didn't understand for squat, but I suspected Pa did not like. Ruby and Gary were examining one row of corn while Pa and I checked the row beside. Out of the blue, Ruby looked over at Pa and fired away.

"With all this saving of animals, you must pay hefty vet bills. Do you have a stash hidden somewhere, Ray?"

"A stash?" Pa's voice was raspy with aggravation. Then he coughed out a laugh, but it was mirthless.

Ruby stared at him, shrugged her shoulders and said, "Just asking."

Pa turned his face away from her, back in my direction since I was about five stalks behind him. His words came out, sort of under his breath, and she probably couldn't hear them. But I did.

"That question doesn't deserve an answer," he muttered. His voice didn't sound like Pa; he sounded like someone I never knew.

All four of us went back to work and for a long time, nothing more was said. Not by anybody, not even Ruby.

If summer gets pretty hot, Pa lets us take afternoon breaks away from the sun. Ruby and I either sit and talk in the shade of a copse of trees on the southern side of the farmhouse, or we sit in the courtyard, under the only tree out there, and close to the fountain. Gary often goes indoors and talks with Ma. There are fans inside, and it stays pretty cool in the adobe house.

Pa tries to keep going, even in the heat. He will take off his shirt, sometimes spritz himself with water, and check or tend to fences or crops or critters. Or he stays in the shade of a shed or the garage, and cleans and repairs tools, or the plow, forklift or truck. But he never plows in hot afternoons because it might be too much for Rufus when he was working, or Jasper, now.

I've noticed that Ruby often waits to see if Pa takes his shirt off, and when he does, she never wants to stay inside the courtyard. She wants to be outside somewhere she can watch Pa while we talk.

In later autumn and for most of the winter, we can take longer breaks, depending on the weather and the critters, and what needs getting done. There's always something. In spite of that, I can remember quite a few 'afternoon-breaktime' talks I've had with Ruby, occasionally with Ma or Gary, too. During breaks, just like when we're working, I don't say much, but I listen plenty.

****

Ruby and me were sitting on smooth rocks in a field that rose from behind the barn toward the apple orchards. We were north of the barn and the hay shed though, so we could see down a little, into the horse pastures. We were watching Rainey and Lurcher grazing in their field when Ruby started talking.

"That right there," she pointed at Lurcher, "that's a lilac and purple horse."

She looked to me for an answer, "Well?" I didn't have much of a say to offer, so I said nothing.

"Okay. Maybe more like burgundy, the color of wine you've never had." Ruby was determined to rope me into this nonsense.

I said, "Never had wine, no. But Pa says Lurcher's part Appaloosa."

"Yeah, he's part Appy, all right. But marbled, mottled, something like that. Looks purple to me."

"Varnish roan Appaloosa. But only part, because of his big head." I just said that straight out, so she'd listen.

Ruby laughed. "Well, la dee dah, girly! Pretty fancy talk from you, I'd say. How the hell do you know that?"

"Pa said."

"Of course, he did."

****

On another afternoon break, we were under the tree in the courtyard. We could hear the bubbling brook sound the fountain made, so I was not inclined for conversation. Ruby wanted to talk, though.

"Know what? I've been working here on Espinosa farm going on three years now. That's near a record for me. Don't often stay put anywhere. Not for long, anyway. Kind of a rover girl, that's me."

After she says something like that, Ruby always looks to me and waits for a response of some kind.

So, I said, "What do you mean by 'rover girl?' I've heard Pa say 'rover' about Dexter, but he's a boy cat. And you're not."

"I mean, I'm a gypsy, Agga," Ruby explained, after she gave me a wrinkled eyebrows expression. "Not an actual, for real Gypsy, like the caravan people. And not an actress in a traveling theatre company. Just a girl who keeps moving. My only home is wherever life takes me. I'm always listening in my heart for when it's time to move on to something new."

"Then you always leave?" I asked her.

"Yeah, girl," she said. "I follow my heart."

This was a serious sort of subject for her, and Ruby's voice was softer and sadder than usual. Whenever I replay that conversation in my mind, I hear the bubbling water in the background.

****

During a mid-afternoon heat break, Ruby and I sat beneath some trees on a slight rise in ground to the southeast of the adobe house. Gary was with us, in the middle, and leaning his back against a tree while he stood up. Us girls were sitting down, Ruby on a curve in a tree trunk, me on the ground.

We all had bottles of water. Gary poured most of his water over his head, and Ruby drank some and used some to wet our bandanas, hers and mine. She dribbled some water through her long, wavy, dark hair, and tied her hair back up on top of her head as best she could. I decided I was lucky to have short, chopped-off hair, not pretty but easier to live with. All I had to do to cool off was push the sides of my hair back behind my ears and let my wet bandana lay against the back of my neck. I drank all my water, slowly, little by little.

Gary was droning on about how his brother Bob was talking about marrying his steady girlfriend. I was looking at Gary and listening to him, and nodding in the places that seemed right to me. I didn't know if Ruby was hearing what Gary said, but I could see that she was watching shirtless Pa cleaning the pickup truck.

Suddenly, Gary got our whole attention, both of us.

"…if that happens, I'm planning to move over here, to the Espinosa farm." Gary spoke this next bit to me. "Think your Pa would be okay with that?"

"Better ask him," I said, flat-voiced to brook no argument.

"Christ, Gary!" said Ruby. "If you move here, it'll be like us winning the lottery! You could start earlier and work later to save us girls the trouble. Maybe you could help Dulce with the cooking. Aggie and I truly suck at any sort of housework, and Ray's always saying Dulce needs the help."

She loves to tease him. Although the part about us girls hating housework was true.

 "I'm serious!" Gary snapped back at her. "So is Bob!"

"Is Bob getting married just so you'll move out?" Ruby would not give him a break.

"He actually loves this girl, 'Miss Smarty Pants,' even if you don't know what that means! When they have kids, they'll need my room. As you'd know if you ever listened to a word I say, Bob is running the Pepper Farm now. And in case you haven't noticed, I'm working over here, have been for years."

Ruby just shook her head and chuckled at him, but I felt for Gary. So, I tried to help as best I could.

"You already have a room of your own in the house, and I bet Pa might like having you move over here. Ask him, is what I say," at the risk of repeating myself.

"I will," said Gary. "In spite of what your friend here may think she knows, I like it here, Aggie. Thanks. I'll go see Keegan right now."

Gary walked off, in back of the garden and in front of the barn, toward Ray Keegan and the pickup truck.

When Ruby made to get off the branch she was sitting on, I stopped her with my words.

"Wait a bit, please, Ruby. Give him a minute. He needs encouragement," I said softly, surprised I said anything at all.

She stayed seated, and smiled at me. "And you'll give him the encouragement, won't you, Agga?"

I didn't answer, just shrugged my shoulders. Ruby looked away from me, and over at Ray Keegan, nodding while he listened to Gary Pepper.

****

One rainy autumn morning, the downpour suddenly stopped before nine o'clock, and the sun came out full before ten-thirty. Pa checked the pastures at noon, and told us it wasn't too muddy for turnout, so we put all the equines in pasture and fed extra lunch hay since the grass was still damp.

Ma kept the chickens inside their coop in the barn though, because it's super hard work keeping chicken feet clean but it's also super important that their feet don't get too muddy and dirty. She waited until midafternoon, after the sun did its drying out work, and then Hombre, Persk and I helped her let them out in the garden, which is protected by the trees and extra netting on top of the screened dome. And later, inside the barn, I helped Ma wipe chicken feet and feathers clean before they strolled back into their indoor coop.

But earlier, right after we fed lunch hay and Pa said we could take a longer lunch break, Ruby grabbed my arm and practically dragged me aside, outdoors, in back of the barn.

"Let's get something to eat and hide out between the southside trees, you know, that place we go to talk. I've got something I need to tell you," she whispered.

I told her, "OK," but I wondered what could be that important that she wanted to get me alone. I soon found out. We put a large towel on ground in the center of trees, ate our lunch, and she started her strange story.

"Remember, I told you that I keep moving around, and that I used to live in Los Angeles. I stayed with some friends there off and on, and we used to visit this crazy place in Topanga Canyon. A rich, older guy owned a house there, and I moved in with him. Sort of. A lot of people stayed there with him, not just me."

I broke in and asked, "Did you learn about taking care of horses and riding in Topanga Canyon?"

"No. That was after I left the Topanga house; that was in Chatsworth and Malibu. But that's not what I want to tell you. If you please, let me get back to the rich guy who liked me and his house I moved into.

"The place was kind of trippy, a crash pad, almost. The guy was a lot older, would never see 49 again and looked it, in spite of dying his hair strawberry blonde. He had a thing about pretty young people, and he liked having them hang out in his house, as long as they'd have sex with him for sure, and maybe do drugs with him. There were parties many nights, when we'd get stoned and drunk, and dance and have love-ins, like. You never knew how many people would still be there in the morning. It was pretty freaky."

I kept quiet and stared at her. I had nothing to say. But she had more.

"Even before I moved in with this older guy, I heard about a sexy young guy who used to hang out at the house in Topanga. Everybody talked about how hot he was, how much fun he was, how much they missed him. The owner, the older guy I was with, showed me a photo of this handsome guy and told me I would have been crazy about him. My old man also told me, this sexy guy never lived there; he would visit every other week and stay a couple of nights. His name was Ray Keegan and his visits were important, actually essential to the owner. Ray brought the drugs in."

"I kind of wish I'd never heard that story," I said. "What are you getting at, really?"

Ruby winced. "Well, you asked about the newspaper photo I saw of Ray. That house is where I saw it. My old man had kept the article that told about Ray getting caught. After that, since Ray went away, the house owner had to find another dealer. After he showed me that picture of Ray, my rich old man and I had the best sex we'd ever had. He even asked me to marry him, and I thought I might do it, cause then I'd be rich."

I let out a big, loud sigh, and asked her, "Why didn't you get married?"

Ruby smiled. "I had to be honest with him. I told him it wouldn't work since I was too dumb and too outspoken to be a duplicitous female, like guys always seem to prefer, but too jaded to be agreeable either."

I hated to ask but she expected it. "What did he say to that?"

"Goodbye."

To my relief and her credit, Ruby laughed first and loudest.

****

Busy winter days are sometimes harder work than planting days or harvest days. On those days when rain pelts down real hard and cold winds blow all day, we have to clean stalls and hand walk the horses and mule inside the barn, one or two animals at a time. And we can't let the chickens or cats outside.

We get drenched, going to and from the hay and feed building, bringing in food for our animals, and trying our best to keep the hay and feed dry. Draping tarps over the hay and feed filled wheelbarrows works fairly well, but even though we wear rain slickers with hoods and work boots, we get wet, and muddy, too.

If it's frosty as well as stormy, we have to protect the crops as best we can. On the rare occasion when it hails, we struggle to put hail netting over the apple orchards unless weather forecasts have warned us the hail is coming, then the netting's up ahead of time.

Even in hard rain, thunder storms, or hail, Persk goes with us, and he gets drenched and covered with mud also. Pa drags a big tin tub into our mud room, just off the kitchen, and fills the tub with warm water to wash Persk off. He doesn't mind his bath, and he loves being toweled off by us, all five of us, taking turns.

It's hard, working a farm in bad weather, but it has to be done. Farms don't close when it's storming outside, and animals have to be fed and cared for every day.

****

One afternoon last winter, when rain and wind stopped around four o'clock, we fed the critters and Dulce made supper early. Ruby had volunteered to clean up the dishes and do night-check in the barn, and Ray took Dulce and me in the pickup to see a movie in town.

The movie was "A Star Is Born," and it was sad, but I loved it, most everything about it: Ally, Jack, Bobby, Ramon, almost everybody really, and Charlie, the dog.

Also, the music! About a month after we saw the movie, Pa and Ma gave me the soundtrack CD, and I still listen to it whenever I get a chance.

Another afternoon, late in winter of this year, when it had been raining off-and-on all day, but not too hard for pasture, Ruby and Ray were out checking fences; and Dulcie, Gary and I cleaned the chicken coop, vestibule, and garden, as best we could. After we finished, I took a break in my room and listened to "Shallow," one of my favorite songs from the movie.

 After I played the song a couple of times, I decided to get a head-start on Ruby for a change and go out to the hay shed to start on supper hay. We would put the hay in wheelbarrows inside the hay and feed building, so equine supper would be ready to bring over to the barn. Usually Ruby was way ahead of me with this, but I figured she'd still be out fixing fences with Pa.

That was the worst decision I ever made.

Because it was rainy outside, a heavy canvas tarp was hanging partway down the middle of the hay building entrance, between double doors propped half open. It was easy to duck under and go inside, especially for me since I'm pretty short, but the hay, feed, and wheat straw for bedding were still protected from getting wet. As soon as I went in, I got a feeling that something wasn't right.

Although it was quiet inside, the air didn't feel completely still to me. And for a second, I thought I heard something, a strange little sound I couldn't identify. But, thinking it was my imagination, I walked carefully behind a tall stack of wheat straw, and went down the aisle left open between stacks of straw and hay bales and the wall on one side of the building.

Toward the center of the building, on the side where I was walking, is where we keep the wheelbarrows. I glanced into each of the three empty barrows sitting there, side by side, but the wire cutter we used to open hay bales wasn't in any of them. Where was the fourth wheelbarrow? I walked behind a stack of alfalfa hay, and then I heard the sound again. Closer.

When I began my turnaround to look behind me, I was facing hay stacked high but unevenly, so halfway through my turn, I could see past the hay. I froze and held my breath. I was looking at Ray's face in profile.

He was facing the entrance to the hay building, but his eyes were closed, and his head was tilted back a little. His lips were slightly open and he was making a very soft chuffing sort of sound.

I was afraid to move for fear he'd see me or hear me. Then I noticed Ruby's hand, partway up Ray's chest. She held up his T-shirt, clenched between her thumb and forefinger, and I could see his skin all the way down to the top of his hips. And see Ruby's arm against his skin. When I looked down, I thought I could see Ray's blue jeans flapped open and also see the top of Ruby's hair. I wasn't sure, but I kept myself from looking down again.

Feeling paralyzed and afraid to breathe, I couldn't move my head or look away. I wanted to look away though, because I knew I should not be seeing this. Or be standing where I was standing, partway hidden behind the hay. I wished I could will myself out of the hay barn. It was almost like that last night in the anger house. I did not completely understand what was happening, but I sure had no idea how to stop it.

Suddenly Ray winced and looked down. He sighed and stepped back, and then I heard him zip up his trousers. I was terrified he'd look my way and see me, but even still I kept my eyes mostly on his face. He wrinkled his forehead and blinked his eyes a little. Sounding like he was short of breath a bit, he pulled his T-shirt down, and then he spoke to Ruby. His voice was low, but in the quiet, I could hear what he said.

"I'm sorry, Ruby Cooper. I wronged you, girl. This should never have happened, but I promise you, it will never happen again. I hope you can forgive me."

With those words, he turned away from her and walked out, ducking under the tarp. I was thinking, 'Ruby Cooper. Don't think I remember ever hearing your last name before.' And while I was thinking that, Ruby stood up.

She was facing away from me, luckily, looking after Ray toward the partly open doors. Abruptly she turned a little and faced the back of the hay barn. Now I could see that her left arm was up and she wiped her mouth on her forearm. Then Ruby buttoned up her short-sleeved shirt while she spoke. Her voice was whispery and sad, as though she was close to crying.

"Why say you're sorry…I was the one who started it. I was the one who wanted it. Always, I wanted you. From the day I walked onto this farm, I wanted you, Ray. I want you, still."

Mortified, I watched her walk farther into the center of stacks of hay, and push the fourth wheelbarrow out into the center clearing. Supper hay was already stacked and the wire cutters were lying on top. Ruby left the wheelbarrow where it was, picked up the wire cutters, and on her way out, I heard her toss them into one of the three wheelbarrows sitting to the side.

I waited a weak, shaky three minutes, I counted, and then snuck out of the hay building. It was dusky out, but not raining, and I headed for the horse pastures. Within minutes, going in the opposite direction, Ray led Jasper toward me. He smiled and nodded to me.

"Bring Rainey next, please Aggie. That'd be good. Thanks. Ruby's getting Taz and Lurcher."

My strides lengthened, and I saw Ruby with the two rascal geldings coming my way. Just as we were about to pass, the timed lighting on the outside of the big barn came on. Before Lurcher blocked my view of Ruby, her eyes met mine.

She winked at me, and then she and the horses passed by. But I knew she hadn't seen me behind the hay; she couldn't have. She never looked my way then. That wink was just her way. Just the way Ruby was.

****

A couple of days later, the rain came down hard for most of the day. At one point in the morning, there was even lightning flickering across the sky. But there was almost no heavy wind, so one of the barn doors was not shut tight, and Ruby held the door open, and she and I looked out from just inside the barn. The darkening sky looked scary but absolutely beautiful.

"Will you look at that, girl?" Ruby said to me. "Is that a trip? Gorgeous, isn't she?"

Conscious that she and I needed to help Ray and Gary finish cleaning stalls, I nodded to her and watched crooked gold streak the indigo sky, over top of the land.

"Mother Nature. How amazing is she! You'd think, wouldn't ya, that the folks in charge should realize that next to her, all their so-called power doesn't amount to even a big nothing," Ruby said as she smiled at me. "But every once in a while, and more often all the time, she shows them. Doesn't she, just."

I said, "Farmers respect her though."

Ruby's eyes teared up; I'd never seen that before.

"That's right, girl. Farmers do." Then she laughed.

"Uh oh, we're farmers; we better get going. We got work to do." And she closed the barn door.

****

Two days after that storm, on a Sunday, the easiest work day of the week, usually we only take care of critters and relax, I was sitting by myself in the sun-dried courtyard, very late in the afternoon. Earlier, around ten in the morning, Dulce and I had played with Anita. Ray had even joined us; he's a playtime powerhouse and can really get a cat, or a dog, or a horse going when he wants to.

But come dusk, after all the farm's animal residents were in the barn or the shed and had their supper, and Dulce and Gary would soon be starting on our supper, I went back out to the courtyard. It wasn't full-on dark yet and I was alone, just sitting there, pulling up a stalk of two of grass to nibble on, and daydreaming and enjoying the evening.

A light came on in Dulce and Ray's bedroom and since their inside door was open, I could see Dulce in there, putting folded clean clothes into a chest of drawers. I was already facing their room so I watched her. All at once, I felt very sad for her, often working by herself although she did have Gary as company lately.

But it wasn't Gary who walked up behind her and put his arms around her. It was Ray, and Dulce's smile became a thing of joy to behold.

Watching this didn't feel bad to me in any way, and I saw Ray hugging and squeezing Dulce, and her, giggling and holding onto his arms. He had put one side of his face down next to hers and it seemed like he was whispering to her. They were paying attention only to each other and did not notice me sitting out in the courtyard. I had never seen them snuggling like this and it made me happy to see them now.

The single worry I had about seeing them together was that I realized Gary had to be making supper by himself. That was the only thing that occurred to me, but I cut that thought off. Nothing I could do about it anyway, and maybe Gary would do okay.

I felt rather than heard Ruby walk up beside me. She didn't sit down, just stopped and stood next to me. We both watched Ray and Dulce for a moment, and then Ruby spoke. Her voice was much softer than usual and strangely full of sorrow.

"Lawsy, lawsy, Agga girl," she murmured. "See how he loves her so."

She stood for a minute, and she put a hand on my shoulder. We looked at each other and smiled, but her smile was sad. Then Ruby turned around and walked away. Probably going back to her room to relax before supper. I sat a moment longer, got up and brushed myself off, and went into the kitchen to see if I could help Gary.

****

Supper was on the table and the main course, I guess you could say, was highly unusual, something we'd never had before, but it looked and smelled so good, I could hardly wait to eat. Had to wait though, since Dulce and Ruby weren't at the table yet.

While he worked, Gary had explained to me in the kitchen what he fixed and how he cooked it and what went into it. He baked fish, orange roughy, in the oven while he blended tomato paste, tomato juice, mushrooms and onion, with a big squirt or three of fresh lemon juice in a saucepan on the cooktop. Then he basted the fish with the sauce he heated up. He also cooked brown rice and put the divvied-up fish fillets with sauce on top of the rice on our plates.

Seconds after Ray sat down, Dulcie bought her supper contributions over. Our large wooden salad bowl contained Dulcie's specialty: flowers, leaves and fruit from her garden. It was nasturtium flowers and leaves with peach slices in a sweet dressing Dulcie makes herself. Next, she carried over a large plate of garden-grown baby spinach sautéed in butter.

We were ready to eat, but still no Ruby, and she was almost always the first one at supper table.

Quick, I said for everybody to go ahead and start eating, and I would go check Ruby's room. She must have fallen asleep; she had seemed tired when I saw her this afternoon. Dulce picked up Ruby's plate, wrapped it in foil, and set it inside the turned-off oven, where it would stay warm. Before I got up from table,

I savored one forkful bite of the fish on my plate.

"Heaven!" I told Gary.

He flushed with my compliment, and I wished I didn't have to go. On my way out the kitchen door to the courtyard, I'm pretty sure I heard Dulce and Ray praising Gary's efforts.

Crossing the courtyard, I could see there were no lights on inside any of the three bedrooms, mine, Gary's or Ruby's. The inside and outside doors allow for a sliver of air or light underneath so even if both doors are closed at night, you can sort of tell if someone has their light on. Ruby's light was off, and I didn't like the looks of that, but maybe she was asleep.

I knocked twice on her door. No answer. I opened the door partway and glanced around. Even before I flipped the light switch on, I knew she wasn't in her bed or anywhere in her room. The air in the room felt vacant, as though someone had drawn all movement and life out. I turned on the light. The bed was made, the closet door was open, the room was empty.

I left the house through the living room and front door and hurried over to the barn. Outside building lights were on so I could see where I was going. Carefully I opened one of the barn doors a crack, then closed it back up. It was dark inside the barn. Ruby would have put a light on; she wouldn't be in there in the dark. I wasn't going to look anywhere else. I knew it was no good.

When I walked into the kitchen through the back door, Persk greeted me and followed me to the table. They were all looking at me, Ray, Dulce, Gary and Persk.

"I can't find her," I said to them. "She's not here."

Ray got up and pulled out my chair. When I sat down, he pushed the chair in closer to the table, and Dulcie got my supper plate out of the oven for me.

"Sit down and finish your supper, Aggie," Ray told me. "I already ate, and I'll take the pickup out and look for her. How long ago since you saw her, are we talking?"

"Over an hour at least," I said.

"Did she leave her things or take them?"

"There's nothing left in her room. Nothing."

He winced and told us all not to wait up; he'd be a little while. Then he picked up his keys by the back door and left. The rest of us went back to eating. I was upset and didn't think I'd have any appetite, but the food tasted so good; I ate everything on my plate.

After we cleaned our plates, Dulce got Ruby's supper out of the oven and we split that up between us. Gary said he'd make her a sandwich and some soup if Ray brought her back with him. I washed and dried the dishes since Gary and Dulce cooked. While I did that, they both took Persk for a walk out in front of the house. We were all very subdued and quiet.

In spite of what Ray told us, we stayed up, waiting in the living room for Ray's return. And we were all still there, even Persk and Anita, when he came back. He was alone.

Ray told us he drove both directions on Sugarhill and back and forth on the highway, all the way to the towns nearby, one to the south, the other to the north. He said he looked everywhere for her, but didn't see her, or any evidence of her, anywhere.

Ruby was gone.

****

During the early morning of the day after Ruby disappeared, all four of us helped put horses and mule out in pasture and fed breakfast to all the critters. Then Ray and Gary cleaned stalls while Dulce and I, with Persk and Hombre helping, let the chickens out. When I joined Dulce back at the chicken coop, she told me she would collect eggs and spot-clean the coop by herself since Ray wanted me to go with him. Gary was going to check fences, the apple orchard, and crop and pasture fields on foot and by himself, later on.

Ray was already in the driver's seat of the pickup when I got in. As he drove slowly out the gravel drive to Sugarhill Road, Ray told me to keep an eye out for Ruby or any of her belongings. He said he would take the same trip he took last night so we could check for her during the daylight. I just nodded; I was too worried to speak.

He took the difficult left off Sugarhill onto the highway, so we could first search in the town to the south of our farm. It was the closer town, and people there knew us and knew Ruby. No luck there, and from there, Ray turned the truck right, back onto the highway, heading for the larger town to the north. He told me there was a small train station as well as a local bus station in the northern town.

That's where we heard, in the bigger town's train station. Ray talked with the man at the ticket office while I sat on a bench nearby and watched. Ray showed the man a picture of Ruby and the man looked and held on to the photo, and got out a cell phone.

While the ticket agent kept his eyes on Ruby's photo and talked into his cell phone, Ray glanced over at me and smiled. He didn't know yet; he just wanted to calm me down.

Cell phone clicked off and set down, photo handed back, ticket agent speaking and Ray nodding, I knew we had some definitive news. I held my own hands and put them in my lap and looked down. In my head, I said a prayer to Mother Nature to keep Ruby safe on her journey to her next place.

Ray sat down beside me and put an arm around my shoulders.

"She got the final passenger train out last night. The agent with the late shift remembers her partly because she ran for the train after she bought her ticket. And probably partly cause she's Ruby. She had a backpack and a duffel bag with her. The guy I talked to said that from her destination, she could go farther north by either train or bus."

"So, she's on her way somewhere?" I asked.

"Yep, she's on her way somewhere," he nodded along with his words, and gave me a one-armed hug. "C'mon, let's go. I'm taking you out to lunch, here in town. I know a place, and we can have lunch before we drive home. Maybe, we can talk about Ruby. Huh?"

I nodded, and we got up off the train station bench. I felt relieved and nervous at the same time. I had never gone out to eat with just Ray before. That I could remember, I hadn't had many, if any, private talks with what I considered adults. Except for Ruby, and she did almost all the talking. I was going to have to talk to Ray and it scared me half to death. Maybe I'd just eat lunch instead.

But no, I had to tell him. We sat across from each other in a booth and ordered. He told me I could order anything I wanted and we might both just as well 'eat up.' I shouldn't have waited to tell what I knew, but I was so hungry, I waited till I was almost finished and Ray was having coffee after he ate.

See, I had made up my mind, weeks before Ruby left. Since I was over nineteen years old, going on twenty, I decided I was a grownup and should try to act like an adult. My Ma and Pa, who weren't really my Ma and Pa anyway, had names. Like I had a name, Gary and Ruby had names, and all the animals had names.

"Ray," I said, and he flinched a little. "I have to tell you something Ruby told me."

He was holding onto his coffee mug like it was a comfort toy. His face looked drawn and worried. He raised his eyebrows as he looked at me.

"Yes, go on, Aggie," Ray said.

"This was about a month ago. Maybe longer. She told me she was a gypsy. Meaning she doesn't have a home; she just keeps moving on, from one place to another. She said she's always been that way. I didn't tell anybody she said that because I thought she might stay with us. Or maybe it didn't matter cause she's a free adult person."

"Uh huh," Ray winced while he poured himself more coffee. "You say she told you this a month ago?"

"At least. She said she stayed at our farm longer than she's ever stayed anywhere. Told me that almost three years was a long time for her."

Ray nodded, and took a drink of coffee, and held on to his coffee mug with both hands. He looked like a sad little kid, and I figured I shouldn't have told him as much as I did. I didn't think of anything else to say so I finished up my lunch without talking.

When Ray went to pour himself more coffee from the carafe on the table, there wasn't enough left for a full cup. He signaled to the waitress for a refill, then rubbed his hands together and seeming more cheerful he made me a great offer that he knew I could not resist.

"Want dessert? How about an Ice Cream Sundae? If it's too cold, you could get a warm drink. Want coffee, Aggie? I'm having more."

No words needed from me; he could see it in my eyes. The waitress brought a fresh coffee carafe to our booth, and Ray thanked her and asked for a mug for me also; sugar and cream were on the table. He motioned to me and I ordered the Sundae with two spoons, please. When we're at home, he always pretends he doesn't want ice cream, and then he always takes some of mine.

The waitress was walking away when Ray showed me his signature quizzical expression and asked me, "You're calling me Ray now?"

I told him about my adult resolution.

"Well, you call me what you want to, but I'll always be your Pa. You know that, don't you? Your last name is Espinosa because of the farm and because Dulce wanted to adopt you under her name, and it was better that way. But you'll always be my daughter, too."

"Okay," I answered. "You're still my Pa, Ray."

His laughter makes me so happy. We both dug into the ice cream and both drank coffee, after I doctored mine, before I looked over at him and said what I really wanted to say all along.

"I miss her already." I didn't need to say Ruby's name; he knew who I meant.

"I miss her, too," he said.

****

That afternoon, after Ray and I got back and Dulce and Gary were fixing supper, I went in my room to look for a book to read. I thought it might get my mind off Ruby leaving. I was trying to choose between "Seabiscuit" and "A Little Yellow Dog" when I gasped out loud.

I had lent "Room" to Ruby so she could read it, but when I searched her room last night, it wasn't there. I figured she took it with her. That was okay by me, I could get another copy someday. But, when I looked next to my William Trevor book, there was "Room," right in its place on my makeshift bookshelf. And a scrap of paper like I use to make word lists was sticking up out of the middle pages of the book.

When I opened to Ruby's marker paper, I saw that she had used my pen to write me a note, something I never expected she would ever do.

Worried, I forced my courage and read.

Agga,
Thanks for letting me read this. I didn't finish, but it's your book and your gift.
Maybe I'll write to you when I have a chance to finish reading someone else's copy, but you know me, so don't count on it.
Thanks for being a good friend to me, girly.
My gypsy heart calls, and I have to go.

Ruby Cooper

P.S. Get Ray to buy you a saddle so you can ride Jasper to check fences.

Fighting tears, I folded her note to use as a marker, closed the book and put it on my bed to start after supper. Then I thought about that "P.S." she added.

Sometimes on cool days when Jasper didn't do any other farm work, Ruby would ride him all along the farm property to check fences. Ray had bought a western bridle and grazing bit at a tack shop and Ruby rode him bareback with that bit and bridle. I remember Ray's instructions to Ruby before she rode out the first time. She was already sitting on Jasper when he said.

"Don't forget, a grazing bit doesn't mean you can let him graze."

"I know that," Ruby had scoffed. "He's not going to graze with me aboard."

"How about when you dismount to tie a marker on a fence, Ruby?" Ray asked.

We used strips of cloth to tie to a fence so we knew which areas needed attention.

"Relax, would you? I'm not dismounting, Mr. Keegan. I won't need to."

Ruby rode Jasper away, and Ray turned to me but spoke to her.

"Well, good luck with that," he muttered.

I had just grinned at him. I knew Ruby. She'd carry extra cloth strips, and after she and Jasper returned, when she put him in pasture or in his stall, she'd wipe off the bit the second it was out of his mouth.

But I also knew Ray. He probably figured that already.

So, I decided I would never ask for a saddle. Didn't want to ride anyway. That was Ruby's thing, not mine. I'd just lead Jasper in halter and rope and let him eat grass for the time it took me to tie on a marker. Exercise and fun for the both of us. And no bridle or bit, grazing or otherwise.

****

Two weeks after Ruby left, Dr. Spelling brought Lizette's previous owner to our farm for a visit with the mule he still loved.

Gary and I were worried that it would be hard to talk with him, or that he'd be disappointed with Lizette's new home, but we were surprised. Thomas, that was the fellow's name, was friendly and easy to talk with. He told us funny stories about Lizette and when he used to ride. And he had so much information about riding, and mules versus horses. We could have listened to him for days.

When Thomas first got out of Joel Spelling's van was heavy though. Ray had put Lizette and Teddy in the temporary pasture so she'd be right in view for Thomas. He walked to the fence and before he called to her, she called to him and walked right up to him. He was thrilled and joined in the laughter. Lizette's voice was a combo of 'whee-hee-hee' and 'hee-haw' and we hadn't heard it that often before.

Since we knew from Joel what day and time Thomas was visiting, Dulce served lunch of homemade vegetable soup and buttered bread, and we ate at the picnic table so Thomas could watch Lizette in pasture. After lunch Thomas said he wanted to stay and groom Lizette but Joel Spelling spoke right up and told him, 'maybe next time.'

While Thomas went inside to use the 'gent's' before they drove back to where he lived, Joel explained to Ray.

"Thomas staying a long time and doing an energetic grooming job – not a good idea. Not at this stage anyway. Might be better when he's had a few more months to recover. Tell Dulce thanks for lunch, Ray."

That was a great first visit and gave us something to look forward to. I feel like we had a second look at Joel Spelling DVM, like maybe even I could talk with him in the future. And Thomas made a surprising first impression. He was so friendly, funny and cute, he has long hair and a character face. Lizette was happy to see him again, she just loves him. But I think Thomas made Gary a little jealous.

Lizette won Gary over and she's become his special pet. He hangs out with her in pasture on some of his breaks and always takes his time grooming her. Plus, he talks to her every time he's near her.

Kind of like I am with Freckles. Only I don't talk much to anyone, but one evening when I was bringing Freckles back to the barn, I stopped him and put my face against his neck, for no good reason. Without knowing I was going to, I cried into his mane a little. He stood there so quiet and patient and nuzzled me. I've always been sort of in love with Freckles, one of our very first rescues.

****

Spring on the way and with Ruby gone, quite a few changes are happening on the Espinosa farm.

Gary and I both work a lot more, that is: harder, him, and a good deal faster, me. I'm handling hay feeds by myself now, morning, noon and night. And Dulcie cares for the chickens and garden by herself, but Gary still helps with cooking supper on most nights.

He lives with us full time now, and it makes a difference. Seems like he has more energy and he's much more helpful with almost everything. He chats with all of us, including the critters, and gets Ray and Dulcie talking more. Once in a while, I even talk with him, while we're working and on breaks.

Ray has been encouraging me to work with the horses more, and Gary doesn't try to butt in, which I appreciate. Ray showed me how to get Lurcher to put his head down for me, so I can halter him and lead him and Rainey out to pasture and back to the barn. Two horses at once, like Ruby used to do. But Ray still handles Taz and Jasper, as far as turn out and bring in go.

Ray used to take Ruby or Dulce with him to our fruit and veggie stand out along the highway or to Farmers' Market in town. He asked me if I wanted to try it this year, after harvest time, but I shook my head no, no, no. Then he asked Gary who said sure. Dulcie and I think Gary will be really good at talking to people and selling our goods. Ray's encouraging Gary, too.

One of the changes I marvel at happened one evening after supper, about a week and a half after Ruby went away. Dulce got out her guitar and played and sang for Ray, Gary and me. That was beautiful and soothed us all.

During her last song, Gary reached for my hand. He

stopped though, and moved his hand back, but he smiled at me a little. I smiled back and made a plan to meet him halfway next time, if he tried again.

****

It's been seven weeks since Ruby left, and planting time is here. Ray and Jasper are plowing fields, starting mid-morning while Gary and I finish cleaning stalls. The extra hardworking days begin as cold weather fades and cool breezes bring fresh scents and liveliness to brighter mornings.

Early mornings, while I'm feeding hay in pastures, I have a little time to think, since knowing how much hay to feed to which animals is automatic for me now. Feeding breakfast hay reminds me of Ruby.

On reflecting back, even though Ruby may have done wild or risky things, and even if she wasn't happy most of the time, she was loved wherever she went and missed whenever she was gone.

I may never find love, of a certain kind, on this planet. I doubt if I will ever be missed like she is, or loved like she was, not now or in the future. And yet, I may be the lucky one because it doesn't seem to matter.

I remember how much the grouchier horses especially loved, listened to, and looked for Ruby. Even now, every morning when I feed Taz his second serving of hay, I catch him peaking around behind me. Glancing quick, over my shoulder, to see if maybe she's there.

He's hoping that maybe his Ruby is coming back to see him, after all.

Yes, Ruby was the one they always loved.

But I was the one who stayed.

NOTE TO READERS

"The Goodbye Station" is fiction, and nothing but.

I am not, and never have been, a horse trainer or riding instructor, or any other kind of horse-related professional.

My only experience around horses has been as an amateur: first, as a horseback riding pupil, and then as an exceedingly lucky horse owner and boarder of three marvelous horses, one at a time. Lucky, because every one of the horses in my guardianship was suitable for me, a close-to-bombproof baby sitter in other words, and all three of them gave better to me than I deserved.

Also, lucky because I found outstanding and suitable horseback riding instructors and took many lessons before I bought my second two horses, and also during most of the time those two horses were with me, and they were with me for the rest of their lives. Plus, I was gifted with quite a few amazing trail riding companions, so important for me.

Although having spent approximately 35 years of my life around horses, riding instructors and horse trainers, stable owners and managers, veterinarians, and other boarders and horseback riding students, I am certainly no expert in any facet of the horse world.

As far as life on a farm goes, I know nothing about it. One of my aunts married a dairy farmer and I visited their farm. My brother-in-law grew up on a farm but what I've learned from him or my sister, or from their son Dan, regarding life on a farm, would not complete even a sentence.

Consequently, please understand:

Everything written in the pages of this novella is fueled by imagination, plus memory, hearsay, and research, but not necessarily by knowledge or experience.

ACKNOWLEDGEMENTS

I want to give thanks, admiration and praise to those humans who treasure, rescue and help animals. They are true heroes to me, those I know personally and those I learn from, through books, TV, movies and hearsay.

My younger sisters are both 'crazy for critters,' all of us are. Patty Bowman, self-acknowledged as 'that crazy cat lady,' adopted and took outstanding care of three four-month old kittens, two brothers and a sister, when a neighbor passed away. They had a forever home with her throughout their lives, and all three lived to be senior much-loved cats.

Likewise, Debbie, our youngest sister, and her husband, my brother-in-law Jake Rowland, rescued four kittens from a farm in transition. One of the kittens was tiny and seriously injured, but let her presence be known to Jake, he brought her home to Debbie and they saved her. That tiny kitten is now happy and healthy and one of four young cats who comfort and are comforted by Debbie, who, along with Jake, also cares for and adores two dogs, and four cows.

And speaking of lots of happy critters, friends Joan and Ingolf Klengler have shared their hearts and wonderfully warm home with horses, dogs, cats (including two feral cats, now affectionate, trusting and loving), and rabbits, the majority of them rescues.

Joan and Ingolf also purchased and provided or found companion or retirement homes for rent horses who were past their prime or unable, for various reasons, to continue their work at the stable where they lived. At least nine horses or more found forever homes with or through the Klenglers.

One of the horses, a beautiful, remarkable registered Quarter Horse mare called Shasta, pre-destined to graduate from rent riders to private owner, became Joan's first horse and treasured trail pony, eventually retired, and happily lived to be only weeks shy of 37 years old!

For more than a few years Ingolf volunteered at German Shepard Rescue, and he and Joan took dogs, possibly difficult to re-situate, home as adoptees.

Jill Grisham, friend and ex co-worker, also volunteered for years with a dog rescue center, and may again in the future. Jill and her mom Dorothy love animals, and have cared for their own pet companions in the past. Other family members currently share homes with rescued critters, including cats, dogs and horses.

My continuing gratitude belongs to friends who share their pets. In addition to Joan and Ingolf, Paula Rincon has always been amazingly generous with her precious cat, the adorable personality girl, Mia. Michelle Pancake and Manny Davis welcomed my sister Patty and I into their unforgettable cat Gato's life. 'Community cat' Gato was quite an individual: funny, brave, affectionate, free, adventuresome, gorgeous and darling, full of character and absolutely the most "chill" cat I ever met.

In her charming and magical brilliantly written novel "The Demon of Raven's Back," Patty Bowman focuses on a fictional charismatic representative of a real-life endangered species. Patty also discovered much treasured book, "Betty & Friends: My Life at The Zoo" (Los Angeles Zoo) by Betty White, at a library sale (Remember them? I pray they return someday). Jill Grisham gave to Patty and me, "Living the Farm Sanctuary Life" by Gene Bauer with Gene Stone, another treasure. And I read and re-read a precious personal gift, Joan Klengler's non-fiction book "Luv'n Horses Losing Fear."

Animal themed television shows to live for include the following, all on Animal Planet: "Too Cute," "My Cat from Hell / Heaven" (with 'Cat Daddy' Jackson Galaxy), "Saved by The Barn," and zoo shows "Crikey! It's the Irwins" (Australia Zoo), "The Zoo" (Bronx Zoo), "Zoo: San Diego," and "The Secret Life of the Zoo" (Chester Zoo in North West England).

Huge thanks to friends and family who support my writing, those already mentioned above, plus the following people, many also friends to animals.

Diana Leonard, who has cared for many precious cats, her pets and others, remains kinder and more encouraging of my writing than I could even hope for.

Thanks to: Mary Catherine Dino (former guardian of

cats even though she is allergic to them), Barbara Harms (cat enthusiast), Dale Lee (dog enthusiast), and my family members Jack and Sarah Bowman, and Ida Mae Bowman (dog guardian).

Bigtime thanks to Jerry Vogler (who was cat guardian to the fabulous Minnie) and gave me so much incentive to write.

Hats off as well to Adriene Harris who has gone above and beyond in her care and devotion to at least three dogs and three cats, including two cats she currently calls, "the demon children."

Extra hurrah to Patty, who read and edited this book, made much valued suggestions, and gave me a supreme compliment by comparing my 'Goodbye Station' book to her 'Demon of Raven's Back' book.

For background info, I researched many websites, most of them very helpful, and some of them, exceptionally entertaining.

ABOUT THE AUTHOR

Although born and raised on the East Coast, GRACIE STELLA COOK has lived most of her life in California, many of those years in the greater Los Angeles area with human and critter family members. She worked in the garment, real estate and radio industries, for non-profit conservation and public transportation organizations, and eons ago as a part-time waitress at a bus terminal adjacent diner improbably called The Terminal Liquor Store.

Besides novella THE GOODBYE STATION, Gracie has written and published three novels: THE SCAVENGING FEW; IN THE HOURS AFTER MIDNIGHT; and STOPPING THE TRAIN; and one other novella, AN EVENING WITH FRANKIE EDGE.